UNLIMITED FUTURES

We would like to acknowledge and pay our deepest respects to the traditional custodians and knowledge keepers of the lands on which this work was edited and produced, the Yagera, Turrbal, Whadjuk Noongar and Wurundjeri First Nations peoples. These lands were never ceded. Always was, always will be.

UNLIMITED FUTURES

SPECULATIVE, VISIONARY BLAK AND BLACK FICTION

EDITED BY

RAFEIF ISMAIL &
ELLEN VAN NEERVEN

 FREMANTLE PRESS

Contents

Introduction

RAFEIF ISMAIL AND ELLEN VAN NEERVEN

Compiled from recordings from April 2021 and August 2021 and edited by Hella Ibrahim.

RAI: Hey sibling, how are you?

EVN: I'm not too bad, you?

RAI: I'm good! I remember telling you when we first started working on *Unlimited Futures* that I wanted this anthology to be a conversation, so I think it's really fitting we're doing the introduction as a literal conversation.

EVN: Such a great idea from you.

1 | ANTICIPATORY JOY

RAI: What drew you to *Unlimited Futures* as an editor? 'My friend, Rafeif, steamrolled me into it' is a valid response.

EVN: [laughs] No, I was really excited. I love the title. The title was the springboard for bringing a collective together.

To have that curation of First Nations voices as well as Afro-Black voices was something unique. Particularly when we really started working on this in early 2020, during an explosion of public consciousness on the Black Lives Matter and Indigenous Lives Matter movements. Solidarity between our different communities is really important, I think, in this evil nation state we live in that doesn't care for our bodies, Blak and Black. I note that the usage of 'Blak' in this anthology's title derives from K'ua K'ua/Kuku and Erub/Mer artist Destiny Deacon's use, which dates back to the early '90s. Destiny gave us 'Blak' to liberate us from the terms of reference settlers gave us.

RAI: I had the idea for *Unlimited Futures* in late 2018. I read *Octavia's Brood: Science Fiction Stories from Social Justice Movements* back when it first came out and it changed my life. I really, really wanted something like that here. I was inspired by books like *Octavia's Brood*, *So Long Been Dreaming: Postcolonial Science Fiction & Fantasy* and other works coming out of the US at the time that were First Nations or Afro-Black, but not both.

I thought it would be great to have a conversation. And what better way to have a conversation than through storytelling? That's the language we all speak, to some degree. At the same time, I was wrestling with my place as someone who's in a Black body, but is a settler, and is also a refugee. All of that was something I wanted to explore, and I wanted to give the opportunity for other people to explore it as well.

For me, *Unlimited Futures* was ultimately conversations and skill-building. Anthologies are such amazing gateways for emerging voices. They can launch a career and, as you know, it's so hard to get into publishing without winning a big prize or creating huge amounts of work. And we're often asked to create work that's taxing to ourselves.

So usually your first published work is a memoir or a personal essay, which are brilliant pathways. But I feel like we are at a time where we can give emerging writers more options than that. All the work we've been doing in these spaces — that you've been doing, that people like Melissa Lucashenko, Maxine Beneba Clarke, Alexis Wright and Anita Heiss and every other artist who's paved the way has been doing — it's given us the opportunity to say 'Hey, emerging writers. You can write to your heart's content in 'genre fiction' and still be published.'

EVN: Definitely.

2 | 'UNPRECEDENTED' TIMES

RAI: How did it feel to be a writer and editor in the middle of an unprecedented global health crisis? Working on a project and imagining the future at a time when creative energies are absolutely exhausted and the future seems so bleak?

EVN: 'Unprecedented', how many times did we hear that? No. This is our reality. This is the world that we're living with as Blak and Black peoples; we're in a constant state of panic and alarm and survival. In some ways, COVID-19 was a very familiar time. It was the dealing with white people losing their shit about their world ending that was so fatiguing. It was such a joy to work on *Unlimited Futures* during 2020 and 2021, because these were the kind of works that I needed during that time.

RAI: I think it's brilliant that our writers created something in such a tempestuous year. There was so much fatigue and fear, and it wasn't an unknown fear. Bla(c)k folk know biological warfare. We know the effects of environmental destruction. Submissions opened and closed in the middle of a major lockdown in the Eastern States, at a time where it was hard to create work. But people still rallied and created. Such a tremendous act of courage, but also such labour. That's really admirable, I think, and just goes to show how much works like this are needed.

3 | RIVERS MEETING

RAI: Our incredible cover artist, Larrakia woman Jenna Lee, created this beautiful cover that looks at the interaction of separate cultures in the most respectful and wonderful way. I love that the cover symbolizes infinity — we're not the first to have these conversations or write these stories and we're not going to be the last. I think this anthology's the continuation of something great, and I love that our cover reflects that.

EVN: We were also really happy that it reflected the movements of water in this work. We were going to begin the anthology with water to allow those kinds of threads of connection and continuation to flow into each other. For me the cover really kind of feels like rivers connecting and the life that is created through water, but is also water that we protect and have a relationship and a responsibility to.

RAI: Absolutely. We begin on water and we end on land as we seek new worlds. Just looking at the table of contents, you can see that it does feel like a river interweaving all these stories. One of the themes throughout this anthology is our responsibility to land, to water, to air, and what we must do to protect that which is precious to us, the responsibilities we've been entrusted with. It's a running theme throughout, whether a story's set in so-called Australia or in a different place.

Another thing I want to highlight is the use of non-linear time throughout the anthology. Our works aren't set in this reality's near-dystopian linear timeline. Instead, you have works that exist in the space beyond and the space before and after, but there's no distinct time. I think that's really, really important to show that, for us, the past, present and future, are happening simultaneously.

4 | UNAPOLOGETICALLY BLA(C)K

EVN: I think when you and I talked about the project early in the process, you talked about how much you wanted it to be for emerging writers. It wasn't until after I'd read and worked on the submissions with you that I understood why you wanted this to be an anthology full of emerging voices — because it's so powerful!

RAI: It is, yeah. I feel like that's what's needed in the literary landscape. Anthologies are these beautiful glimpses into what people can do as creatives, without having to produce an entire book right off the bat.

EVN: It's incredible to have a strong percentage of emerging voices sitting beside established voices. We opened submissions and we didn't know what we were going to get. We didn't know who would submit. It was incredible to read those submissions and just be blown away by writing that is so different. The new authors excite me the most because this could launch their careers or be a significant moment for them. With the established writers, there's a kind of assumption that what they're going to send us is amazing, but there's an added excitement to reading work by someone who's unknown to you and making a connection with them.

This type of writing can be a hard genre to break into as an emerging writer. I think a lot of people hadn't seen a call for submissions quite like ours before, and they'd been waiting for it. Creating a home for that, for this space, was exciting. I love that we opened it up to poetry. Where else do you see a call out for speculative visionary poetry?

RAI: And including a mixture of prose and poetry shows that speculative or science fiction doesn't have to be written in one style. We start the anthology with a poem; it's a really powerful thing, I think, to start with a poem. Then we go on to short stories, then another poem, and it works. It works so well.

EVN: We tried to look beyond the writing and publishing norms to create something that's very global as well. We have writers representing so many different countries, First Nations and cultures, something that's sort of beyond what was possible here in form and in the content.

RAI: Absolutely. And accessibility was kind of central to everything in this project. We made it explicit in the calls for submission that yes, these works can be multilingual, they can be recorded instead of written, etc. I think that made all the difference.

All the stories in this anthology are written for Blak and Black audiences: the language used is unapologetically Blak and Black, the absence of the leering white gaze is a palpable relief. It makes it so much more powerful. That's what makes *Unlimited Futures* unique.

EVN: I agree. That's what's exciting about this work. It makes no apologies; it gives no explanations. Sometimes our communities feel like they have to write for a certain audience, sometimes there's a pressure as a First Nations writer to represent all First Nations people. We wanted to free writers from those pressures. And you know, we're more powerful as a group, so to have this kind of a critical mass of writers representing Afro-Black communities and First Nations communities means you don't have to be just one person. Each story represents a different aspect or narrative, then they join up together.

RAI: These stories are dismantling the idea that First Nations or Afro-Black folk are a monolith. I love that speculative, visionary works aren't … please correct me if this is wrong but I feel like, at least in African cultures, they're not speculative. Speculative isn't the word; it's just another reality. And what better way to start a conversation between our communities than at the root of it all?

It's just so beautifully interwoven. We're seeing that with how the pieces in this anthology interact with each other. The commonalities, the differences, the hopes and dreams and the fears, but also the calls for action, the calls for change. *Unlimited Futures* is one conversation in an ongoing dialogue. And I think it's brilliant that we got the chance to add to that dialogue.

I also want to acknowledge how incredible the process has been from the beginning. Everything was handled by First Nations and Afro-Black writers. I think it's really important we centred our voices, and we made sure our voices stayed centred throughout the entirety of the process.

5 | PARALLEL QUESTS

RAI: You know when you pick up a story and you read it and you just … smile? That was kind of the feeling for every single one of those final submissions, wasn't it?

EVN: Definitely. I'm so happy that we had this gathering of stories and we also have some of our established writers, like Sisonke Msimang and Alison Whittaker, writing in genres that they haven't written before. I wanted to point that out, because I think that is a beautiful thing in itself. Feeling like they had the freedom to explore an idea beyond their usual kind of output is really cool. This genre of fiction is often seen as the poorer cousin to realist fiction or other types of writing that are seen as more literary or more serious or whatever. But genre fiction is so fundamental to our storytelling and our worlds, and it's about time it gets the recognition it deserves. We have works of genre fiction written by Aboriginal and Torres Strait Islander writers and Afro-Black writers that were ignored by both the literary establishment and the mainstream, works that are now out of print or very hard to find. In doing this work we honour those writers, and we also honour the writers who had a fantastic story but never had the opportunity to be published.

RAI: Absolutely. And in saying that, I want to highlight that 'The Prime Minister', the piece that closes this anthology, was written in 1945.

EVN: I still can't get over that. What a moment to hear about this writer, who's no longer with us, but wrote this amazing gift. It's almost like finding a message in a bottle or something. Incredible to think about Aboriginal and Torres Strait Islander writers and Afro-Black writers creating these kinds of stories in the '40s and earlier than that, and it being so relevant to today.

RAI: Exactly. It shows that our parallel quests for liberation have been ongoing, too, it's not just this recent thing. When we engage in activism, we're imagining new worlds. We're establishing new worlds. And that's what we do when we write visionary and speculative fiction. We imagine new worlds so that we can build them.

'The Prime Minister' perfectly encapsulates that feeling. This is a piece written in the 1940s, based in Queensland, that dreams of space flights and the first Indigenous Prime Minister and this sort of almost utopian Australia, free of colonial chains. I can't get over how beautiful that vision is and how badly it should become a reality.

EVN: I just felt like I was sitting on something incredible. A piece that was going to change the world when it was published. To be publishing a story by an Elder who's no longer with us in the living world, his story of imagining a better country … it blows my mind to think about how many of our ancestors were writing visionary fiction, telling stories about a different, better, future world. So many of those stories we will never see, but I feel like it's deeply known that they have been told and that they're out there.

I'm really grateful the family allowed us to publish this work, and that they've been able to take care of it and to recognise its significance. I can't wait for people to read it.

I have a feeling it could open up doors for other families to be like, 'Hey, we've also got this story, our ancestor was a sci-fi writer'. There were so many barriers for First Nations people to publish any work seventy-five years ago, let alone science fiction — it's such a gatekept genre, and the political power of these stories would have been too much for white people back then to handle. Maybe people today, too. It's still too much for them to handle. I just hope this piece encourages people who know of relatives with stories that also need to be told.

RAI: I felt really humbled by 'The Prime Minister'. This story was written the year the Second World War ended. My own country was still colonised in 1945. We still didn't have independence. Most of the world was still under some sort of colonial rule.

The hope for humanity that's in this … in the end, humanity is what visionary fiction is all about. It's the hope that we *can* and we *should* do better. Most of the stories in this anthology are about actions and consequences, how we can alleviate those consequences or how we can survive them. The consequences of imperialist, capitalist, white supremacist cis-heteropatriarchal society is the reality that we're living in. There's a lot of talk around depoliticising 'The Arts', but art is always going to be political; 'The Prime Minister' is a political piece of work. Works like this are pockets of resistance.

6 | UNLIMITED FUTURES

RAI: I can imagine *Unlimited Futures* being read ten years, twenty years, fifty years from now and still being a powerful body of work. What do you think this genre will look like ten years from now?

EVN: I think we'll be seeing a lot more of this writing over the next decade. Genre fiction is already vital writing, but I think it'll become even more vital as reality becomes more and more unstable with everything that's happening, politically and environmentally. We're going to need to pass the tools of visionary resistance down to the next generation and check in with our older generation about it as well. Things are so unstable, and storytelling gives us power. This is what our ancestors have always done — used storytelling as a way to imagine a better future and to have that conversation with the past as well.

RAI: We can see that power in this anthology already. And what I love about it is every single one of the stories *does* move towards justice in the end.

EVN: I absolutely agree. Justice is a key thing. We're moving towards it.

RAI: I want to mention a few of the people who supported us through this project. Maxine Beneba Clarke, who helped champion this anthology; I had conversation after conversation with her being like, is this viable? How do I write a letter, asking a publisher? Maxine was incredibly generous with her time and amazing advice. Leanne Hall, who helped facilitate one of the very first letters of support. Ambelin Kwaymullina and Rebecca Lim, who gave us *Meet Me At The Intersection*, Melissa Lucashenko, who was so supportive of this project and who, along with so many great authors, shaped the literary landscape for us. We also had such great support from Hella Ibrahim at Djed Press, the team at Fremantle Press, and more people than I can name honestly. It was absolutely a community effort. *Unlimited Futures* could never have been something created and sustained in isolation.

EVN: I feel like I can't wait to give them the book and say like, 'thanks so much for your help, and for laying down the foundations for us to do this work'.

RAI: And thank you, too. I've been so excited to work with you! Your wealth of knowledge and experience has been so absolutely lifesaving, all the times I would come and be like, 'hey, what if we did this?' And you're like, that's not sustainable. Or 'so what is X, Y, Z?' And you'd explain it. It was just such a beautiful experience. I know they say never work with friends, but I'm so glad that we were friends before we worked together. I don't think I would want to do a project like this with a stranger.

EVN: I wanted to thank you as well for your incredible vision, and your openness. I hope that this is just the first of many collaborations between us and the other contributors in this book.

RAI: Same here! It has been an amazing journey.

Rafeif Ismail and Ellen van Neerven
with Hella Ibrahim
October 2021

UNLIMITED
FUTURES

The River

TUESDAY ATZINGER

In the savannah, near a mighty River, lay a great village
They were the people who slept under the sun
Prosperous
Ubuntu
Together
The waters of the River ever roiling under the heat
Shallow water so clear that the stones beneath it glistened brightly
Depths dark and mysterious, hiding all that lay below
The River ever a source of sustenance

And of danger

Eons ago
The River had rippled in welcome as the people first arrived
Provided refuge as they began to build their huts
Lapped against the stones as the people huddled over crackling
fires after dusk
The River had seen passion, grief, joy and courage
As the village grew and prospered

The River had heard whispers, laughter, the clucking of
chickens and the lowing of cows
The wails of every woman and the mewls of every newborn
The River's waters washed over the backs of the people, fed
them, slaked their thirst
It allowed its waters to dance wildly around splashing children
held close by worried siblings

The River flowed beside the village
Of the people who slept under the sun
Ubuntu
Together
Shallow waters friendly and inviting, offering up glittering
treasures
Depths dark and mysterious, a veil to enshroud all that lay below
Its waters ever a source of sustenance

                                        And of danger

The River had borne witness to a lineage of Chiefs
Some wise, some brave, some imperious, each falling way to
another
And now it rested its gaze on Mehluli — the Warrior Chief
Proud, powerful, commanding and eager

                        Arrogant, violent, dominating and greedy
Born near the River under the moon
First-born and destined to rule
Mehluli reigned with open arms and a clenched fist

Kind words and a dextrous tongue shrouding a yawning hunger
Ambitious outstretched fingers demanding more
Shrewd words translated into benevolence through gleaming teeth
All at once the piercing prick and soothing salve
He held himself with an honour and nobility spoiled by greed
Hollow and hungry
A facade of righteousness and virtue
Nothing could satisfy his aching belly
Not tribute from the people who slept under the sun
Nor conquest of the tribes
pulled into the undertow
of his want for more
The ebb and flow of his desires
neverending

And so the coursing River bore witness to the Warrior Chief
The village of the people who slept under the sun
A people spent from war, weary and wary
Prosperity coming with a price sombre and heavy

The swirling waters of the River also testified to love
A love known and envied throughout the village
A tender, soft love shaped by fingers climbing over one another
A tremendous love echoed in laughter over a shared fire
A pure love stoked by open embraces and fluttering kisses
Thandeka and Amandla had such a love
Their eyes seeking each other in hidden moments

A love woven together each night with every caress come nightfall

Amandla was a hunter
Her shoulders wide, her gait sure
Her feet steady as she threw her spear
Her hands effortless as she skinned her spoils
Her return almost always a triumph
Her strength burned like fire

                                        But she held only one fear

Amandla feared the River
She feared the darkness and the eddys
She feared the undertow
And the unknown that lay beneath it
A product of a childhood terror that a cold hand would come
And pull her down into the gloom
Even now, when necessity took them to the bank
Even now, with Thandeka's hand entwined with hers

                                        She feared the danger

                                        But danger came anyway

Mehluli's ravenous eyes alit on Thandeka
Her unrivaled beauty calling to his insatiable hunger
And when Amandla was on the hunt
Thandeka could feel his weighted gaze upon her
Knocking against the love she and Amandla had built
An insistent, unspoken intrusion

The Warrior Chief summoned Thandeka to his hut
His desire for her shameless and unrelenting
He offered her the finest blankets and jewellery
His generosity marred by his artifice
But Thandeka thought herself cunning, and refused his finery
She had a lover, she said, and she could not receive his gifts
Mehluli smiled his double smile, and waved her away from the
entrance of his hut
She walked home, her legs trembling, for she knew nobody
could refuse the Chief
And he was determined to have her

The Warrior Chief summoned Thandeka to his hut a second time
His craving for her brazen and unceasing
He offered her goats and cattle
His generosity marred by his artifice
But Thandeka thought herself cunning and refused his finery
She had a lover, she said, and she could not receive his gifts
Again, Mehluli smiled his double smile and waved her away
from the entrance of his hut
She rushed home, her legs trembling, for she knew nobody
could refuse the Chief
And he was determined to have her

The Warrior Chief summoned Thandeka to his hut a third time
His urge for her unrepentant and persistent
He offered her a new homestead

His generosity marred by his artifice.

But Thandeka thought herself cunning and refused his finery

She had a lover, she said, and she could not receive his gifts

Again, Mehluli smiled his double smile and waved her away from the entrance of his hut

She ran home, her legs trembling, for she had refused the Chief thrice now

Nobody could refuse the chief outright as she had done

And he was determined to have her

On a cold evening, with dusk creeping over the horizon

Mehluli visited Thandeka and Amandla as they sat over their fire

He wished to go on a hunt, he said, and he commanded Amandla to join him

Amandla warily gathered her hunting gear

And kissed Thandeka on the cheek

Just as the last vestiges of sunlight kissed the furthest reaches of the land

Mehluli waited patiently outside, biding his time

The pit in Thandeka's stomach dragged her voice down into a whisper

'Stay safe. Stay careful.

Come back to me, my love.'

Amandla allowed herself a guarded smile

She could not refuse the chief

The hunt had been unsuccessful, and as they returned

The moon rose up over the quiet village
Amandla clenched her fingers around her spear
                    Mehluli had taken her to the edge of the waters

He walked into the river, chest deep, and beckoned that
Amandla follow
But she stayed near the bank, thinking of cold hands and dark
depths
Thinking of Thandeka and his double smile
As the stones beneath her feet glimmered in the moonlight
Mehluli beckoned once again
But she stayed near the bank, thinking of cold hands and dark
depths
Thinking of Thandeka and his double smile
As she bathed herself in the shallows
Mehluli laughed, and swam out of the river, his skin wet
Turning her back to him and towards her home
Amandla didn't see his gaping hunger stretch out to swallow
her whole
He stretched a powerful arm across her chest
And stretched his powerful hand across her mouth and began
to drag her to the depths
Amandla was strong, the Warrior Chief stronger
The frenzied struggle churned the water

And then
                    There was

And Mehluli walked out of the water alone

And in the darkness
In the depths
In the murk
The water began to swirl around Amandla
'Do you wish to die?' The River Spirit asked
'No,' Amandla answered into the pressing darkness
'I have been shackled to this River for eternities
I was here before the people who sleep under the sun
I have watched friends and I have watched enemies
I have overseen the lives of everyone
I have slept and woken with you
Ubuntu
I have rippled across each stone
I have been here all alone
But I want more
Allow my water to douse your embers
Take my place
So I may wander from shore to shore.'

'Yes.'

And so, under the moonlight, the River welcomed a new guardian
And an old man, wizened and bent, left the water and walked
into the brush
Unseen by anyone but the River he left behind

And as Mehluli slept, he dreamt of the lapping of water

Thandeka awoke to an empty hut
Discomforted, she searched the village
But nobody had seen her love since the night before
Foreboding loomed over Thandeka like a shadow
Smothering hope
Besieged with distress, she sought out the Warrior Chief
His tongue curled around a lie
Unsuccessful
He and Amandla had parted ways after swimming in the river
The darkness of the lie suffocated all hope
For Thandeka knew that Amandla feared the River

Thandeka returned home
Thinking of the Chief and his double smile
Tendrils of dread snaking their way around her heart
For she knew Amandla
And her love would not swim in the River she so feared
The lie still ringing in her ears
Vestiges of hope giving way to grief
She knew the Warrior Chief had severed her love
Her tender love, her soft love, her raging love
And crushed it beneath his heel
Because she had refused him
And he was determined to have her

Spirit awash with sorrow
Thandeka wept
Heaving sobs that shook the bones beneath her flesh
She would never again feel fluttering lashes on her cheeks
She would never again gather Amandla into her arms
The fiery light in her life extinguished
Her cries soon gave way to the gnashing of teeth
Her fists so tightly clenched, her nails drew blood
Her fear of the Warrior Chief giving way to an atrocious loathing

Misery muted
 She vowed to shatter Mehluli
To splinter his lies in his throat
She discarded all her softness
And steeled herself
Thandeka began to plot
To make him choke on his own hunger
For to her, now, he was but a bloated man
Her hatred rose with the moon
She would mangle him
Destroy him

                                        Devour him

And as Thandeka remade herself
Mehluli dreamt of the lapping of water

The next day, Mehluli summoned Thandeka to his hut
His desire for her bold and unfaltering

He offered her jewellery and blankets

Goats and cattle

And a new homestead

'Your lover has abandoned you,' he said, 'and you cannot refuse
me any longer.'

But Thandeka was cunning and refused his finery

'I cannot accept your gifts, for I am without a lover

And have nobody to enjoy these spoils with.'

Mehluli smiled his double smile, and waved her away from the
entrance of his hut

Thandeka walked home, vengeance within grasp

She had refused the Chief once more

And he was determined to have her

That night, as Mehluli dreamed of the lapping of water

The River rotted

Rancid water rising up past its banks

Dead fish with white eyes floating under the moonlight

The water rolled against the huts closest

And flooded them inside

And when daylight came, and the village of the people who
slept under the sun awoke

They saw that all who had touched the water had sickened

The villagers ran to Mehluli

Lamenting the turning of the River

For a moment, Mehluli thought of his dreams of lapping water

A moment brushed away by arrogance

And he ordered the villagers move their homesteads further from the river

And tend to their sick

As the river had always looked after the people who slept under the sun

And would not forsake them now

But the sick would not heal

They would not eat

Nor work

Nor rest

Silent tears pouring from glassy eyes

traced rivulets across their empty features

Bodies swaying in tandem with the blighted water

The afflicted sighed lifelessly about cold hands and dark depths

About devotion devoured and sacrality submerged

About the cold

About carcasses gutted by the light of a shared fire

And carcasses stirring in the silt

Undeterred by the efforts of their families

The sick soon began to stagger toward the rotten River

Ensnared by its silent, sinister summons

For days they stood near the fetid water

Enchanted by its macabre adornments

Disfeatured fish with ragged scales and cloudy eyes

Snared on darkened water weeds

Mehluli watched on
As his people begged and dragged and offered muti
wailing invocations to the sacred and supernatural
But in answer to their anguished chorus
Fathers, sisters, infants, cousins, the childing
All possessed by a savage thirst
Knelt for the first time in days
And desperately drank the cloudy water, ignoring interfering arms
And filling their bellies beyond nightfall and past daybreak
Before rising to their feet, still weeping,
As the dead air carried their hollow whispers
Of cold hands, dark depths, gaping hunger
Cold hands, dark depths, gaping hunger
Cold hands, dark depths, gaping hunger
Nothing
Come back

           Nothing
           To me

                        Nothing
                        My love

Then whorls of water circled over drowning bodies
As they embraced the River and disappeared into the deep.

Through their mourning
The people who slept under the sun
Began to whisper that the River was cursed

And shunned the sepulchral waters
But Mehluli held steadfast
Ignoring his dreams of lapping water
Ignoring the keening of the villagers who slept under the sun

Thandeka visited the Warrior Chief in his home
Her heart dark with hatred
'Have you come to refuse me once again?' he asked
'No,' she answered. 'If you will take me as your wife, I will be yours.'

Enchanted by her dark skin and seductive features
And thinking himself in love
Mehluli agreed

That night, as Mehluli dreamed of the lapping of water
The rotted River once more rose beyond its banks
Flooding the huts of those closest
And sickening more of the people who slept under the sun
Weeping
Standing
Staring
Kneeling
Drinking
Whispering
Drowning

The few who dared to venture close to the River

Told stories of limbs lying prone atop glittering stones
Of sunken bodies staring at the sky, eyes unblinking
And soon the villagers pressed their strongest and bravest
To collect their loved ones from the water
So they could lay the profaned to rest
Before long, those chosen by Mehluli
Tentatively approached the River
Careful not to succumb to the blight
Slowly, they reached out for the limp hands at the River bank
But as soon as Mehluli's chosen touched skin
Once insentient fingers clenched tight over outstretched arms
And onlookers watched helplessly
As the water churned violently, and all who had ventured too near
Were pulled mercilessly into the gloom by cold hands into the
dark depths

Once more the villagers called upon Mehluli
Who thought once more upon his dreams of lapping water
And deciding it was an omen
Ordered the villagers to move away from the rotting river
Away from the village that slept under the sun
And deep into the savannah under the shaded trees
Satisfied that he had outwitted the river
Mehluli took Thandeka as his wife
The ululating of the weary and wary people subdued

Thandeka poured Mehluli beer all night

A shrewd ploy to avoid his embrace
Patiently, she waited for him to fall into the arms of sleep
Her eyes on his spear
But Mehluli was troubled by the river
And did not succumb to the depths of slumber
So Thandeka, heart cold, bid her time

The next morning the people who slept under the sun awoke
To find the rotted River had followed them deep into the Savannah
And sickened more of them
Again, the people lamented to Mehluli
Who was grasped by terror at the sight of his people
Void and sighing, embracing the dark, stinking waters
He ordered his soldiers find a sangoma
To rid the river of its curse.

Many sangomas tried to unravel the mystery of the River
All of them succumbing to the rot and sickness
All except Sibakhulule
Sibakhulule was both old and wise
Her face wrinkled and weather worn
She sat at the edge of the River, fearless
The people who slept under the sun watched on in awe

As she suddenly sat up, and walked into the befouled water
The waters swallowed her up, rippling first before they stilled
The villagers looked on for hours, hope dwindling

Before the waters began to undulate and Sibakhulule emerged

She fixed her gaze on Mehluli
And recited what the River Spirit had told her
'I was a hunter, strong and proud
Until I was untimely drowned

                    I seek to pull my love to the deep
                        Her beautiful face to see
                            To wrench her away
                        from the one who killed me.'

A cold hand gripped Mehluli's soul
'We need to move far, far away from the river,' he decreed
'It is cursed.'
Sibakhulule shook her head
'The River will follow,' she said
But Mehluli was adamant, and sent the sangoma back to her tribe

The air around the village was cold
Though none dared defy Mehluli
His crimes were now open to all
And the villagers began to whisper among themselves

That night, plied by beer, Mehluli sank into the depths of sleep,
dreaming of rapids that buoyed him this way and that
Before a cold hand pulled him into the black
Thandeka, gripped by hot rage, took a heavy rock
And raising her arm, smashed Mehluli in the head

He awoke, vision bloodied, and fought her off
'Why, my love?' he shouted, rousing the villagers
But Thandeka struck him once more, teeth clenched to cracking
'I exist only to destroy you
As you once destroyed my perfect love,' she spat

Vengeance demanding satisfaction
But before she could strike again, the villagers subdued her
                              And began to drag her to the River
For it was her the River wanted, not the people

Mehluli looked on at all he had wrought
'Baba, what have I done?' he cried to his ancestors
His hunger was no more
Nor his double smile
He saw himself as he was
A husk of a man, no more than those that had sickened
He had led his people to ruin
For lust, and greed
For his aching belly
He raised his hand, and the villagers stilled
Thandeka still within their grasp

And the people who slept under the sun watched
As the warrior chief, who had lost everything
Walked into the River.

'Do you wish to die?'

'No.'

The waters stilled, then stirred, as Amandla walked out
All the sickened villagers in tow
The River had a new guardian

In the savannah, near a mighty River, lay a great village
They were the people who slept under the sun
Prosperous
Ubuntu
Together
The waters of the River ever roiling under the heat
Shallow water so clear that the stones beneath it glistened brightly
 Depths dark and mysterious, hiding all that lay below
The River ever a source of sustenance

And of danger

Fifteen Days On Mars

AMBELIN KWAYMULLINA

Day One

It had been almost a year since we came to Mars. That was what I called this place although it had another name. It was Kensington Park or Windsor Estate or something like that but I couldn't have said what because I could never remember it.

I hadn't wanted to come. But we'd all agreed that Mum couldn't go alone and when the time came to decide who would go with her my brothers and sisters had looked at me. Fair enough, I supposed. I was the only one without kids and none of us thought it was a good idea to bring children here. We knew what it would be like to be the only Aboriginal people in Settler suburbia. So it was just Mum and me on Mars. And like always, I was doing the weeding.

I'd started wrestling with the weeds the day we arrived and I was nowhere near to winning the struggle. I'd managed to liberate one small corner of the front garden and establish an outpost of wildflowers, my first foray into bringing back the plants that were here before the Settlers came. But everywhere else was covered in the towering stalks of the pale, glittering weeds. The scent of their flowers burned my throat and their leaves were so cold they froze my fingers and the barest touch of their thorns drew blood. But worst of all were the way the roots multiplied and spread and if I didn't get every last one the weed didn't die. Each day I pulled up tiny root after tiny root beneath the hostile gaze of my neighbours. Weeds grew in their gardens too but they found them to be beautiful. They tended to them lovingly and called them roses.

A shadow fell over me. Mum.

I sat back, wiping sweat off my face with my arm and looking up at her. She was holding a cup of tea, which wasn't surprising because Mum always had a cup of tea. What was unusual was that she wasn't drinking it. Instead she was staring across the road. I shifted, following the direction of her gaze to find she was looking at the couple moving into number eleven.

The man was the sort of person who you could tell usually wore a suit even when he wasn't wearing a suit. Right at this moment he was dressed in crisply pressed slacks and an open collared shirt. He was talking on his phone. It was left to his too-thin blonde wife to direct the movers, which she mostly did by screeching at them: be careful, don't put that there, do you have any idea how valuable that is, don't touch that it's delicate … Apparently everything they owned was enormously valuable and very special. Sometimes she glanced at her husband, perhaps hoping he'd scream at the movers too. But he just frowned in irritation and continued speaking into his phone.

I looked back to Mum to find she was still staring.

'What is it?' I asked her.

She shrugged. 'Dunno.' Then: 'Maybe someone who can see.'

'Them? Are you sure?'

She didn't say anything else. But Mum wouldn't get something like this wrong.

I sighed. 'Guess we'll have to get to know them, then.'

Day Two

I slept in. Again. I was finding it harder and harder to muster the enthusiasm to get out of bed.

I showered and dressed, wandering into the kitchen to find Mum had made biscuits. When we first came here she'd visited the whole neighbourhood with biscuits. I'd tried going with her but it hadn't taken me long to get angry with the people of Mars.

I was angry with the ones who began every second sentence with the words I'm not racist but … I was angry with the ones who kept inviting us to parties just so they could show their lefty friends that they knew some actual

Aboriginal people. I was angry with the ones who wanted to save us and the ones who wanted to steal our lives for some book they were writing and the ones who droned on and on about some bullshit journey of self-discovery that was just endless Settler navel-gazing. They were all so unbelievably ignorant it was hard to keep from shouting, although it hadn't taken me long to figure out that I didn't actually need to shout for most of them to believe I had. If I spoke to them in anything but the mildest tone of voice they reacted as if I was the one who'd taken something from them. Then they expected me to make them feel better.

Mum didn't get angry, or sad and exhausted either, at least not like I did. I'd asked her how she did it once. She said she was older than me and closer to the generation who'd had to live like this their whole lives. And what we were experiencing here wasn't the worst of what happened in those times. It wasn't even close.

Mum was a lot better at surviving on Mars than I was.

I watched as she piled biscuits into a tin. She pressed down the lid and slid it over to me. 'You better get going.'

I stared at her. 'You want me to go to number eleven? By myself?'

She nodded, turning away to put the kettle on. Mum wasn't one for wasting words.

'But … I'm not good at this! You know I'm not.'

She went to the cupboard and took out a mug.

'I'll just get into an argument and you'll have to go over anyway.'

She cast a thoughtful gaze out of the window. 'Weather's starting to turn, I reckon. It'll be cooler today.'

Which was her way of saying she wasn't going to discuss this any further. I rolled my eyes at her. 'Fine. But don't say I didn't warn you!'

I grabbed hold of the biscuit tin and marched it over to number eleven. There was no car in the driveway. The Suit has gone to work. Maybe the too-thin blonde had too. For a second I let myself hope that no one would be home. But when I rang the doorbell, someone came.

Close up she was even thinner than I'd thought and less perfectly presented than I'd expected. Her hair was a little frazzled and dust was clinging to her clothes. I guess even she couldn't manage to move house without getting a bit grubby.

I forced my lips into a smile. 'Hi. I'm Billie. From across the road?' I held up the tin. 'I bought biscuits to, um, welcome you to the neighbourhood.'

'Oh. Thanks. I'm Sarah. Please come in.'

I followed her into a house decorated in shades of white and beige, just like every other house on Mars. Except …

I paused at the edge of the living room, casting a curious glance over it and into the kitchen beyond. Things were in disarray and it wasn't just the mess of moving. There didn't even seem to be much mess of moving — boxes were stacked into tidy rows and clearly marked in precise handwriting. What had happened here was something else. Every drawer in the kitchen was open and all of the cupboards too. The cushions of the couch were overturned and pale throws that I'm sure had been artistically draped were piled into muddled heaps on the floor.

'Are you looking for something?' I asked.

She laughed a high, brittle laugh. 'I'm such an idiot, I can't find the keys to the house. My husband called to remind me to check we had a key for every lock and I was sure I put the keys on the counter — they must be in here somewhere …' Her voice trailed off and she twisted her hands together.

'I could help you look, if you like?'

I expected her to say no. I couldn't imagine Mrs-don't-touch-that-it's-fragile would want someone poking around her house. But her face lit up. 'Oh, would you? Could you check the kitchen again? Maybe you'll see something I didn't!'

She must really want to find those keys.

I trotted into the kitchen, setting the biscuits on the counter and making a show of glancing about. I was genuinely looking, but not in the way she thought. My great-great-great-great-great grandfather had been a legendary tracker who could find anything or anyone. I'd inherited a sense for lost things.

The keys had been on the counter, all right. But now they

weren't in this room at all. I glanced over at Sarah to find she was flat on the floor, peering under the couch. I shrugged and followed the energy of keys. The trail led me down the hallway, into the master bedroom, and to a set of drawers beside the bed.

There were four drawers in total. I opened every one and rifled through. No keys. But I was sure they were here. I searched again, more carefully. This time my hand brushed against a set of rolled up socks that jangled when they moved. I unrolled them to find the keys inside.

I gazed at them thoughtfully. My sense for lost things sometimes extended to lost people. I should have realised yesterday but I understood Sarah now. She'd been shouting at those movers because she was afraid of what would happen if anything was less than perfect. I wondered if she really cared about things like artistically arranged throws at all. I wondered who she was beneath the person she'd had to become.

I rolled the socks back up, shut the drawer, and returned to the lounge. 'Found them!'

Sarah shot up from the floor. 'You did? Where were they?'

I should probably lie and pretend what was going on in this house wasn't what was going on in this house. That seemed to be what people did on Mars. But I wasn't from here. 'They were in a drawer. Beside your bed. Inside a rolled-up pair of socks.'

'Oh. Um — I remember now, I had them when I was unpacking socks last night.' She laughed a laugh that was even higher and more brittle than before. 'I must have rolled them up by accident. How silly of me!'

I handed her the keys. 'I think you put them on the counter.'

There was a small, airless silence. Sarah's gaze slid away from mine and for a second I thought she might be about to say something real. Something true. But then she lifted her chin and smiled a smile as false as the one I'd worn when I first came in. 'Well. Thank you for your help — it's been wonderful to meet you, but I have so much to do, I'm sure you understand what it's like …'

In other words, get out of my house. 'Yeah. I'll see you around the neighbourhood, I suppose.'

I made it as far as the middle of the road before I had to stop to get a hold of myself. I was so furious I was shaking. But I couldn't do anything about how people lived on Mars, not unless they asked for help. And she'd just thrown me out.

When I trudged into my own house the air was filled with a familiar scent. Mum blended her own tea and the one she'd just brewed up was meant to be soothing. She always knew when I was upset.

I climbed wearily onto a stool at the kitchen bench and Mum pushed a steaming mug across to me. I took a sip, then another. I was halfway through the cup before I could find any words. Then I told her about how the Suit had hidden the keys and made his wife look for them, setting her a test he knew she'd fail. I didn't know what the punishment was for failure but I could guess.

Mum sighed. 'So that's how it is then.'

'Yeah. That's how it is.' I took another sip. 'Still think there's hope for them?'

She snorted. 'Not for him.'

No. This was about her. 'I made a mistake.' I confessed. 'I let her know that I knew what he was like. People don't do that here, do they? They pretend. Or they don't notice at all.'

Mum was quiet for a moment. Then she said, 'Don't reckon it was a mistake. Not if you felt it was right.'

It had felt right. But I didn't trust my instincts, not here in this upside-down world.

I'm sure you understand what it's like ... But I didn't.

I didn't understand Mars at all.

Day Three

Someone was shaking me. 'Wake up!'

I blinked my eyes open. 'Mum? What's wrong?'

'She's coming over.'

'Who's coming over?'

'The woman! Number eleven. Get up.'

She gave me a last shake and left the room.

I scrambled into clothes and hurried out to find Mum

standing in the lounge, peering through a tiny gap in the curtains.

'What are you doing?' I asked.

'Watching.'

Ask a stupid question … I walked over to her so I could look out as well.

'Sarah's not coming over,' I said. 'She's just standing outside her house.' Except she was holding the biscuit tin.

'She's making up her mind. But she'll come.'

Sure enough, Sarah began walking across the road.

We both leapt back from the curtain. 'I don't know what to say to her, Mum! I messed it up yesterday.'

'You'll know what's right.'

I didn't think I would. But when the doorbell rang, I answered. 'Hi, Sarah.'

'Hi. I was just — that is, I brought your tin back.'

'Thanks!' She probably threw those biscuits out. I'd bet the Suit didn't let her eat chocolate. But I didn't say that out loud. She looked nervous enough already and I didn't want to scare her off.

Mum reached over from behind me to take the tin from Sarah's grasp and fill the air with words. She always used a lot of words when she spoke to Settlers. 'Oh, you're Sarah, it's wonderful to meet you, I'm Iris, Billie's mother. Now you two girls go sit on the patio and I'll bring you some tea. Go on now!'

We didn't have a patio. We had a carport. But we also

didn't have a car so Mum had put a carpet on the concrete and a table and chairs on top of the carpet and rainbow lights up above.

The two of us sat down and I searched for something to say other than the thing I actually wanted to say, because telling her to leave that bastard who was beating the crap out of her would probably send her running back home, never to return. Finally, I came up with, 'How are you liking the neighbourhood?'

'Oh, it seems very nice. I haven't had a chance to meet many people yet, but I'm sure we'll love it here.'

Well, that hadn't gotten me very far. Now it was my turn to say something else and I had no idea what. I'm not good at this.

Sarah blinked at me. 'Not good at what?'

I'd said that out loud. I opened my mouth to lie and realised there were no lies left in me, not that there'd been many to start with. I'd never had to lie back home. Do what feels right, Mum had said.

Well, okay then.

'Look.' I said. 'I'm not good at talking about nothing. Where I come from, it's okay to sit and be quiet. People don't speak unless they have something to say.' Then it dawned on me that she might think that meant she couldn't talk at all and I added hastily, 'But of course if they do have something to say, I mean if you do, then you should say it ...'

I stopped before I got anymore tangled up than I already

was. I had a sinking feeling today wasn't going any better than yesterday.

But Sarah's lips curved into a tiny smile and I realised it was the first real smile I'd seen from her. It reached her eyes and none of her other smiles had.

'Sitting and being quiet sounds good to me,' she said.

I gave her a real smile of my own.

After a while Mum came out with a tray that held two cups and an enormous teapot. She put the tray onto the table and vanished back inside as the sharp, spicy scent of the tea surrounded us. The blend for strength.

We drank two cups each and never said a word.

Days Four, Five and Six

We sat in silence, and drank tea.

Day Seven

I'd just finished weeding when she came over. The results of my labours lay at the edge of the carport. A single weed, torn from the ground. It had taken me a week to get it out and it would take me another half a day to cut it up into small enough pieces to fit in the bin.

As I sipped my tea I realised Sarah was looking at the weed. My grip tightened on the cup as it occurred to me that she might want it. The weeds were resilient. They'd grow again if you put them back into the ground. I'd learned that the hard way after the neighbours had started taking the ones I dug out and planting them in their gardens.

Her gaze shifted from the weed to me. Her mouth opened. I braced myself for what was coming.

And Sarah said, 'I fucking hate roses.'

I laughed so hard I snorted tea out my nose.

Day Eight

We were on our third cup when she spoke, 'I want to say sorry to you. For everything my people did. I want to tell you that I know my world grew out of what was stolen from yours. But I don't know how to give it back and if I can't do that what does sorry mean? I am sorry. But it's not a big enough word.'

Day Nine

She didn't come.

I waited and waited. Finally I went over to her house and knocked on the door.

Nobody answered. I knocked louder.

Still no answer.

'Sarah! I yelled. 'I know you're in there. Come out!'

There was the sound of footsteps from inside and the door opened, although not all the way. She wasn't bruised any place I could see but I could tell from the way she was holding herself that she was in pain.

'I can help you,' I said.

'Go home, Billie.'

'I—'

'Go home.'

She began to close the door. I jammed my foot in it. 'Listen to me. Just imagine … imagine …' Imagine that this world is all a lie. But I couldn't say that without breaking the rules and anyway it wasn't a lie, not to her or to anyone else who'd lived in this time. Instead I said, 'This land is old. Older than your people. You know that. And for thousands of years, my ancestors were women of power. So just … think about that. If I could help — if you were sure that I could help — would you ask me?'

A long silence. Then a whisper. 'Yes.'

I moved my foot and let her close the door. Then I raced home and repeated the conversation to Mum. 'She asked!'

Mum gave me a long, steady look.

'Well, she as good as asked.'

'Good enough for you and me.' Mum said. 'But for them upstairs?' She shook her head. 'I don't know.'

I didn't know either but I hoped. I hoped all the way through the rest of the day. But when night fell and nothing had happened I knew Mum had been right.

I stalked outside, glared up at the night sky, and shouted. 'It's not a fair rule!'

But of course there was no answer.

Day Ten

Sarah didn't come over and when I knocked she called through the door for me to leave her alone.

I tried again a few hours later and then a few hours after that. She sent me away every time. I went home, got into bed, and curled into a ball.

It's not a fair rule. Living on Mars made people smaller by degrees. How could someone ask for help when they didn't believe something better was possible? And anyway Sarah had asked. Only it hadn't been direct enough. Not for 'them upstairs', which is what Mum called the Blue.

Blue wasn't really their name. But we perceived them as aqua coloured mist and they seemed content to be known as the Blue to humans. The truth was we knew very little about them, except that they were some kind of intergalactic healers. But we knew why they'd come. It was because of the Fracture.

If the Blue understood what had caused the Fracture they hadn't shared that information with us. What was certain was that something had smashed into the relationships that were space-time and cracks had spread out from the point of impact. Now bubbles of the past were floating across my reality. The Blue were directing all their resources to repairing the Fracture itself so it was left to humans to do something about the bubbles. Except we had to follow their rules and while those rules weren't always fair I had to concede there were reasons for them. Shifting people between contexts when they weren't ready for it could cause their minds to collapse.

Mum had been one of the first to sign up for the job of changing a bubble-world, or at least changing some of the people enough so that they could exist in our reality. I was just here so she wouldn't be on her own. Or that was what I told myself. But sometimes when I was alone with my thoughts I had to admit that maybe the reason I got so angry with the people of Mars was because I was so disappointed in them. I was so disappointed for them.

The door creaked open.

'I don't want any bloody tea,' I growled.

'It's not for you. It's for me.'

It wasn't but I didn't argue with her. Mum sat on the end of the bed and took a loud slurp, as if to prove the tea was hers.

I buried my face in my pillow and did my best to ignore her.

'I've been thinking,' she said. 'We could ask.'

I threw the pillow at the wall. 'We did ask! Or Sarah did. The Blue didn't do anything.'

'Wasn't thinking of talking to them upstairs.'

'There's no one else to talk to!' I snapped. But the second I said the words I realised that there was. 'Wait, you mean her? But … Sarah's not related to us. She only does things for family.'

Mum shrugged. 'Might be, she'll make an exception. This is a strange place we're living in. Strange times we're living through. I reckon we could try.'

It was a chance. Not much of one, maybe. But a chance.

I sat up. 'Give me the tea.'

After I'd finished the cup I went into the backyard to make a fire in the firepit and Mum went into the kitchen to make more tea. When the fire was done the two of us sat by the flames, sipping a brew so strong it was almost bitter. I winced at the taste but I drank it anyway. It wasn't a moment for weak tea.

The stars were out and the night air was cold. But the shivery feeling I was experiencing had nothing to do with the weather. I had to tell Aunty Mary's story. The women of my family had been doing this for generations, all the way back to Granny June. But I'd never been the one to tell the story before.

Mum picked up the poker and leaned over to stir the fire with it, sending sparks spiralling upwards. Then she nodded at me.

I drew in a breath and began, 'Aunty Mary was born into hard times. The cruel times, when the government took the children.'

I made sure I spoke in a soft voice. I didn't want to surprise Aunty by saying her name too loudly. It wasn't wise to startle someone so old and dangerous.

'Aunty Mary got stolen by those government people. Her sister got stolen too. And the children's home they put them in …' I let my voice trail off and shook my head, just as Mum had done when she told me the story. 'It wasn't like any of those places were good places. But this was one of the worst. The boss man was a hard-hearted man. And the women who worked for him were even harder.'

Something moved in the distance. I stopped talking for a moment, taking a sip of tea and tracking the movement. But there was nothing there. Except I knew there was. Somewhere far away, someone had turned their head towards us.

Aunty Mary was listening.

I swallowed and continued. 'They made the girls wear hot, scratchy dresses. Those dresses had pockets and Aunty Mary would hide things in hers. She made a game out of it for her sister June and the other little ones, tucking away flowers or leaves or stones for them to find. But one day those hard-hearted women saw her playing the game. They yelled at her for getting her dress dirty and made her scrub the pockets until her hands bled. Then they took her to the boss man and told him she was a grubby girl who didn't know how to live in a civilised way. And that boss man beat her.'

I stopped again and took a big gulp of tea. It was harder than I'd thought to speak of the cruel times. The words were heavy on my tongue and my heart was pounding.

Mum patted my arm, letting me know I was doing okay. I kept going.

'Aunty Mary was scared and sad and she hurt all over. But most of all she was angry. She was so angry her body wasn't big enough to hold it. So she got bigger. She grew until her head was in the sky and her shadow stretched across the land. She grew until she was so big that she could have squished the boss man and the hard women just by stepping on them. Only she didn't do that.

'She picked them up instead. And she put them in her pocket.'

When I was a kid that had always been my favourite part. I liked to think of Aunty Mary tucking the bad people away where they couldn't hurt the children. I still did.

I took a last mouthful of tea and finished the story, 'And sometimes, if you listen in the right way, you can hear that man and those women crying: Mary, Mary, let us go. But she never will.'

The stars disappeared. I let out a yelp of alarm before I realised what had happened. The stars hadn't gone anywhere. I just couldn't see them.

Mum and I were in Aunty Mary's shadow.

In the total darkness the fire seemed to burn unnaturally bright and the air was thick with the presence of power. Mum found her voice before I did. 'I've been thinking about the woman who lives at number eleven. Sarah. That man she's married to …' Mum sighed. 'He's a bad man.'

She nudged my foot with hers and I knew I had to speak. 'She — she's not family.' Because Aunty Mary usually only did things for family and I wanted to make sure she understood we were asking her to make an exception. 'But she's ... she's ...' My mind went suddenly, horrifyingly blank, and I needed Aunty Mary to know Sarah. Say something! I screamed at myself. Anything!

Words came rushing out. 'Sarah knows how to share the quiet. She doesn't try to fill up every silence with things that don't need to be said. She understands something about how to be sorry. She knows the roses are toxic, and that's not something that people here know.' I stopped. I couldn't think of anything else. Well, perhaps one more thing. 'She's my friend.'

For a second nothing happened. Then the pressure in the air disappeared and the stars came back.

Aunty Mary was gone.

I sagged into my chair. 'Think she'll help?'

Mum shrugged. 'Up to her. Don't reckon she's decided yet.'

I managed a nod, although it was an effort. Telling the story and talking to Aunty Mary had drained me and I wasn't going to be able to do much of anything for a while. I tipped back my head to stare at the sky. The stars stared back. Or maybe the Blue did.

'I guess if she does do something, the Blue might be angry.' There weren't actually any rules about what our ancestors could do in the bubble-world but I'd bet the Blue would want them to be subject to the same restrictions as us.

Mum snorted. 'If they've got a problem, they can take it up with Aunty Mary.'

Day Eleven

Mum and I sat up all night, tending the fire and waiting. When the sun came up we moved into the lounge, pulling back the curtains to look out at the street. For a moment I thought nothing had changed. But then I caught a glimpse of something on the road in the distance. It vanished if you stared right at it. But if you just looked from the corner of your eye, it almost seemed like ... a shadow.

The street began to wake. People walked their dogs. Put out their bins. Went to work.

The Suit came out of number eleven.

Mum and I pressed close to the glass, watching as he got into his car and drove off down the road, just he did every morning. Only this time, the Suit drove into the shadow.

And vanished.

I blinked and kept looking, wanting to be sure. But I'd had it right. There was no more Suit and no car either, although I could still hear the faint whine of the engine. Or maybe I was hearing something else.

Mary, Mary, let me go.

But she never would.

Days Twelve, Thirteen, Fourteen

Relatives and the police descended on Sarah's house. She managed to get rid of the relatives fairly quickly; the police lingered a little longer. They went up and down the street, asking everyone what they'd seen.

When they knocked on our door, we told them we hadn't seen anything.

Day Fifteen

I was digging a root out of the ground when someone spoke from behind me. 'Thank you isn't a big enough word.'

'Thank you is two words,' I pointed out.

I sat back and looked up at her. She'd put on some weight although she had a way to go before there was enough flesh on her bones. Perhaps Mum could make some more biscuits.

Sarah tipped her head on one side. 'Are you telling me you don't want to be thanked? Because I know it was you.'

It wasn't but I couldn't explain about Aunty Mary. 'Where I come from, we don't say thank you. If someone's in trouble, then other people are supposed to do something about it. It doesn't make sense to thank people just for living how they're meant to live.'

'Where you're from doesn't sound much like here.'

I sighed. 'It isn't.'

There was a long, comfortable silence. Then Sarah looked

down the street towards where the shadow had been. 'I was coming to see you, on the day my husband went missing. I was just waiting to make sure he'd gone to work. So I was watching him drive away. I saw … I saw him disappear. Literally vanish. And since then …' Her gaze returned to me. 'Since then, it's like the more I think about this place the less sense it makes. It's not real, is it?'

Well. I hadn't expected her to see that much. But now that she had I wasn't breaking any rules to talk to her about it. On the contrary, once people had started down the pathway of understanding we were supposed to encourage them. 'This place is a reality. But if you're asking if there's something beyond this, something better — then, yeah. There is.'

'And that's where you're from.'

'That's where I'm from.' And that's where she could go, because if she knew enough to question this reality then she'd be able to adjust to mine without her mind falling apart. I squashed the selfish part of me that was sad I wouldn't be seeing her for a while. 'Have you checked your mail today?'

'My mail? No. Why?'

'I think you'll find there's a ticket there. For a flight. If you get on the plane, you'll be taken to where I'm from.'

She didn't seem to be as happy about that as I'd thought she would be. 'But … you'll still be here?'

'Not forever. But for a while.' There was no way Mum would leave now we'd had some success. And I wasn't sure I was ready to go either. I waved my hand across my garden. 'I've still got to clear all this.'

Sarah cast a thoughtful gaze across the weeds. 'That's a lot of roses.'

'Yeah.'

'Guess we better get started then.' She dropped down beside me, picked up a trowel and started digging out a root.

I gaped at her. 'You're staying? But— '

'But what? You're allowed to help me but I'm not allowed to help you?'

'I just meant — it'll be better for you …'

Her eyes flashed. 'This is what I want. And I get to decide what I want. Now.'

I couldn't argue with that.

We worked side by side through the afternoon. As evening approached Mum came onto the patio and put a tea tray down on the table with an unnecessarily loud thump. She thought we'd weeded long enough. Sarah and I made our way to the patio, weary and happy and covered in dirt.

We drank tea together and watched the sun set on Mars.

Night Bird

CLAIRE G COLEMAN

Too afraid to sleep, too tired to be awake, I drink to drown my sorrows, I drink to break my own heart.

I am haunted by the ghost of my Ancestors' Country like a phantom limb; I can feel it sometimes like it's still there; like I am still there with them. The presence of my phantom homeland won't leave me, won't leave me alone. When I wake up it's watching me.

I have been cut off from my Country, my ancestors cut up, the land drilled and dug and eaten by machines. The spirits, the mambara, the animals, are dispersed; my wounded homeland won't let me rest. My mind wanders as I stand in line at the supermarket, one and a half metres behind, one and a half metres before, one and a half metres, one and a half. I hold my thoughts back as they try to flee to my ancestors; I keep me in the moment; I drag my mind into the labyrinth in the pit of my self.

The cry of a night-bird pursues me as I pay for my groceries and leave, as I am packing the reusable bags full of food in my rust-bucket, as I am ignoring a message on my phone; as I twitch turn the key; start the engine, which drowns out the songbirds, the song, my breath with her noise. In my car I am away from the everything, the air, the voices coming with the breeze, the first smatterings of rain blowing in from Country.

Or is it tears? I am crying for the phantasm of the life I never had; the life I could never have, my Country severed. I fear that I am going mad again, I fear that what I am haunted by is myself.

*

I remember the time I returned to Country, the trees and animals gone or imprisoned, the rivers rancid and still, the djildjit all killed dead rotting. The wadjela had carved into the bones of my demangka, digging for stuff they could do without, slaughtered our boorn, our waitch, our worl. I could feel nothing and none of my ancestors, were they dead? Was I cut off?

Attempted Countrycide.

Since then I have always felt my Country like a ghost that

hurts me.Like a phantom limb, it hurt me sometimes,
I could feel the sea breeze on the beaches sometimes,
sometimes I could hear the wind through the leaves and
sticks. From time to time I wished I could be rid of it, never
feel it, see it, know it again, I would rather not know it was
there if I couldn't have it back, rather be cut off completely
than to be this haunted. Only sometimes. Other times I held
onto it like that faint phantasm was what defined me.

Is what haunts me my dead homeland?

*

I wake in the morning and eat a breakfast I don't really want,
put on clothes that fit but feel like they don't, flat shoes that
feel like six-inch platforms and glasses that are suddenly,
overnight, the wrong prescription. I grab my keys and
drop them, pick them up and drop them again. Someone is
laughing at me and I am not sure it isn't me. My guts are full
of concrete and my legs are too long as I climb into my car.
I drive to my studio like I am drunk, stop when I send the
dumpster crashing into the wall with a crunch, sit shaken on
the comfortless seats.

I can hear a voice but I can't make it out. I can hear a song but
I can't catch the words. I can hear the wind and it's stealing my
breath. I can hear nothing and it is screaming.

Nothing is right. The paint has the texture of wet chalk, the canvas is as smooth as glass, the air between me and my easel is as thick as treacle, the air in my lungs is full of broken glass. My phone rings, I drop it when I try to get it out of my bag, it skitters across the floor and under a bookcase full of shit and paint and crap. By the time I find it, reaching for the song with my hands, hoping the spider that lives there under that furniture is not home, it has stopped ringing.

I wait interminably for it to ring again while paint dries and cracks on my fingers but whoever it was decided not to call back. There's a whisper in my right ear but I can't quite make out any words. Someone is breathing for me and they are bad at it, they can't keep the right rhythm, breathing in when they should be breathing out and out when they should be breathing in.

As much as the feeling of my Country is part of me, I want to be rid of it, I want to be like everybody else, oblivious; but I cannot be free. I put my phone down and when I do it feels like someone else is doing it. I feel too large for my skin.

*

I walk into the night and …

Night has oppressed me, and I am inside the night alone but

for my ghost, alone with myself, there is no sound but the breathing of air conditioners, the faint push of wind, coming from the wrong direction — away from Country. I can feel it again, that phantom presence, that wordless voice wanting to talk to me. I try to shake it off, I want nothing of it, wish to be free of it; it's an irritant, a scratch, like a missing piece of my soul tearing at the barbed wire and broken glass that remains where I was torn apart. More than at any other time in my life I feel torn asunder, itching and wrong, aching and lost, heartbroken and afraid.

I slink in the shadows between the streetlights, and something is wrong with me, I am a beast with a mind torn, an animal with a missing limb, a limping, knife-edged, lurching creature, peg-legged, leprous, staggering, unhinged. I am irritated, I am an irritant; I am a bacteria in the veins of the city that has grown like a coral, stitched together like Frankenstein's creature, over somebody else's land.

Something says a word to me and I can't understand it.

Something touches me on the shoulder, I startle-jump terrified and there's nothing there.

Something breathes on my lips, I am shaken.

There's a word on my tongue and I don't speak that language.

The ghost that haunts the soul of me stretches out. I can feel a treasonous part of me reach out with the phantom and touch …

The wind changes, it caresses my back, and suddenly it's coming from Country. Footsteps not my own are brought to me by that new, strange, familiar wind.

I turn to face the sound, small weak fists ready, not knowing what good they will do. A large man-shaped figure resolves out of the darkness and I realise I should not have been walking alone in the night, the rain and the ghosts. Fear assaults me as he approaches, I am far from small but he is huge; he is clenching and unclenching his hands.

Ice is running down my spine, adrenaline is making my heart thump. The whispering voice is back, the place where my soul once connected to Country is itching. I feel like I am standing on a mound of bones. I don't know if I will be fast enough if I try and run with the bones tripping me up; I know I will not be strong enough if I stand and fight.

Something squeezes my heart.

'Child,' a voice breathes to me in a language I didn't know I understood, 'it will be okay.'

'Don't try and run,' pours from the man shape's mouth.

I don't, I try and walk away calmly, hoping my bravado will be enough to give him pause, I can hear his footsteps as he follows, I know I am dead.

The ground is moving beneath my feet, I can feel it shrugging, it shoves me and then I am riding it like a wave not knowing how, knowing I can't possibly keep my feet and surprised I somehow am. My phantom-limb Country is hurting like a bitch and I worry I might swoon from the pain. 'Do not fear, child,' a voice says and I fear it.

I hear the cry of a night-bird, high and long like a wailing lost child, like a heartbroken mother.

I can smell salt air and wildflowers.

I can feel the air embracing me.

Someone screams then grunts, it sounds like a man, I turn around and my pursuer is fallen, the pavement near his feet is buckled. The land is rippling around him like something alive, like an earthquake, like the top of a bowl of barely set jelly. There's a greasy feel to the air and when I turn to walk towards him the air holds me back.

In a language I didn't know I understood, and am certain I will not understand later, a voice says, 'child, you think you are severed from us, but we will always be with you.' I close my eyes squeezing out tears. 'You are always welcome back.'

My phone rings and this time I don't drop it, I push the button to answer and hold it to my ear. All I can hear is the sound of waves crashing against stone and the cry of a night bird. I tell Country I am coming. I hang up and book tickets, I don't need to pack, Country will care for me.

Bridge

ALISON WHITTAKER

Super Street Fighter II crashes if you go too hard. Try telling
Bridge, all balled fists. When he'd punch each button, one
for low attack, one for high, he'd sweat without finesse. You'd
sometimes catch a stray armpit hair, a glance. Such was the
benefit of the scoop-side Jay Jays singlet.

Zyzz he flexed earlier when we were buying tokens,
indicating the swoop from nipple to waist. Bridge did
not have the physique of Zyzz // Russian-Australian
bodybuilder, YouTuber and soon to be heart attack-haver //
but we entertained it. *Anglo geek Zyzz.*

I liked the way his belly protruded a little on his skinny
frame, the tell-tale navel indentation, the exaggerated
nakedness, a crease beneath the pec. The little double chin
on his wrist as his hands pounded that arcade machine. Low
low low high block forward forward low high high.

The pheromones, I resolved to myself. It was the pheromones, grotty little armpit droplets encased in mid-air, that transfixed me in his reflection. Grunting. Effortful. Full.

It is not 1993 // famously, the release year of this arcade game and when we were both born // but when this happens it is 2010 and when I am writing about it to remember // to remember it *as it really happened* // it's 2032. It's weird how through little objects of technology we can situate a time — when maybe the easier thing would be to situate how far behind my family was to get it.

Bridge, though, had time to master it. He'd been training since 1993 for this very moment. *No, that's unlikely.*

//

I came home and asked ngaamba if she ever played *Super Street Fighter II. What do you reckon? I was busy nursing you my boy!*

When my mother talks about 1993 she talks about the perm she had to get in her fringe every few months because it was finally in. She'd spent so long pressing it to an ironing board that her natural coils wouldn't take a curl anymore. Each perm sagged. Holding me up as a baby in photos, her belly not even deflated yet, you can see the sad droop just above her eyebrows.

In 2010, I've got a heavy-set solid black fringe that swoops half my face. It was in // in 2007. But I'm nothing if not a late adapter, once things have filtered through city internet and then rural internet and then to Kmart and then to Salvos.

I liked my mother's caution when I told her about going out with friends from school. *But why the arcade? Isn't it a bit … old?*

In fairness // I'd only just gotten a PS2 // we still didn't have even dial-up // so on our technological scale an arcade was not old at all. Wandering into the school library to get into Bebo proxies to talk to Bridge was enough to get me banned, and now next to no communication other than texts on a Motorolla Razr (even then, ancient) were the only connection I had outside of our family.

With little else to do that felt like it wasn't the fifties, we went to this arcade. It opened to service the late blooming scene kids of the north west // It opened above the old segregated cinema // It opened to Bridge's pale fist, pumping down again and again over the place where he'd get to sit to watch *Jedda*. Me, slightly to the side, with my pathetic little yearning.

//

When we were younger, at the end of the school year, Bridge and I curled up on the floor of his homestead. A week away was a luxury, even just up the namaay. I was astounded his family owned something so big when my Nan and Pop's home next to their river was so small and hard-fought. I later resented Bridge for his wealth, at the time I just nursed this slack unknown feeling in my arms. Whatever, this memory isn't about that.

It was about Bridge's very big TV and the night that his mother came home and said *Something's happening in Sydney.* We turned on the TV to see the Cronulla Riots, white fists pumping down. Bridge's mum turned the TV off, grimacing.

That's terrible. Why would you want to watch that? // and // *Okay boys! Who wants dinner? We can get KFC?* A pause, she and Bridge stiffen decisively in their arms and necks to not look at me.

//

When my mother talks about 1993 she talks about getting in a fast car with my dad like Tracy Chapman. It's to get me to the hospital. She talks about the panic, being so far from it, waiting for a coal train to slip from the north to service the south // slicing this town in half.

I couldn't fathom her young pregnant age when I was at the arcade. I'm not thinking about a fast car, I'm thinking about this shit old game and Bridge's armpits. We were both 17. Is that how she felt when *Super Street Fighter II* was new, hormones surging and hot in the chest, when I became part of her young life? Did she look at it through catalogues or hear about it from friends like I first looked at iPhones, a PS2 // pornographic flash games at Bridge's house? If she did, I felt sorry for her. If she didn't // it was because of me.

When she talks about Bridge in 2023 her mouth is uncharacteristically thin.

I don't like what that boy did to you.

And what did he do to me, Mum?

She pauses. We both suspect she doesn't have much future at this point. She makes the calculation in her mind. *He made you mean.*

//

It wasn't until 2014.

Bridge finally pushed me to a wall and those stupid pheromones did what they came there to do. It was okay, but his hands were too familiar to be titillating, his voice already thick with embarrassing gaffes I remembered from our youth (slapping my dick in the changeroom // *Nice clapstick, mate*). How many other parts of him were invisible to me in my pursuit of this, my clapstick in his mouth? His hands were soft, big and forceful, but they were clumsy. His kisses were dominant without an offering. His jaw felt limp against mine as he heaved *You close? You close? I'm close.*

I was angry. The idiot was ruining it. I slipped my palms around him. I shoved him into the mattress, head first. He laughed with his thin lips and wiggled. *Okay big boy* // an assent to this charged act. We were nearly done with this sweaty switch when he abruptly jerked up // pushing me to the floor with those white soft fists. I lay there // spread out and stunned.

Bridge put his foot on my belly. *You know, that's not how this is gonna work.* I could barely breathe but in acknowledgement, all over my stomach and his ankles, I hissed and came. Bridge wiped it in my hair.

We play a video game after (it's not *Super Street Fighter II*) and never kiss again. But it really happened // But he marries up // But we don't stop this.

//

When it comes time to destroy Bridge's technology, I do. I was two years into a PhD, my mother was still grasping at her life without apology for her prolonged exit. He came up with it in 2026.

Bridge was braiding my hair with some vintage Remington braiding wand. I still recall his tug on my ponytail when he rushed to his desk. Something popped exquisitely in my stiff neck, pained from a night of unceremonious pummelling, but Bridge don't notice.

He's writing something down outside my view. Were we talking about something? About my mother's memory.

I had said *She says she wishes she asked more questions when they were going. Do you think I should too? I don't want to treat her like a library that I'm trying to collect while she just dies. She's her own woman. She has agency, rights, yeah, dignity? I want her to feel supported, not … extracted.*

Bridge paused with his notes in the corner // *Same. I've heard so many stories … about the homestead. You know, my great great grandfather. Surely there's so many more accounts?! I'd like to know it —*

My braid was beginning to slip out without his fists gripping it. I reached out to grab it and he looked up. We made eye contact for the first time that night // but he's not really looking at me.

— *as it really happened* he whispered.

//

From that weird little braided yarn, Bridge's technology itself is pretty nondescript. Enough people have stored stories in it by now, spoken them into some hardware made in partnership with an industry body headed up by Bridge's father-in-law. It collated those stories — and within them, their plausibility, emotional cues, existing data, descriptions, whatever — and turned them into rendered versions of events based on its assessment. He showed it to me in 2030 — by then it was a final prototype. He'd found his friends and family's recounts of mundane enough things and put it in to render // *Do you want to see?*

Sure!

A graduation ceremony at our high school. Bridge emerges dutifully to receive his handshake, long-lashed and beautiful. I follow at the end of the alphabet, sallow.

I guess it wasn't a good day. I turned around in my headset.

Bridge, there's no audience here.

I've had trouble putting everyone in. They don't really … see themselves I guess. Just what's … on the stage

Makes sense.

Bridge and me in a crowd of other miscellaneous teenagers move to opposite edges of the stage for photos. Some flashes from bulbs that I know are not rendered yet. I blur out.

Maybe it's just some bad data. I whipped the headset off, his face to the right of mine and his breath shaky.

Can I try another one?

Bridge's eyes widened. He grinned. *Do you like it? Okay, okay, wait wait wait I think you'll like this one.*

It's us playing *Super Street Fighter II*. He wins, repeatedly // as I remember, aggressive, sweaty, barely clothed.

I asked the staff he said, and I could hear him rubbing his ring finger against the heel of his palm. *And um that group of kids. Cunts to track down, I tell you. They'd all moved out too.*

And, you know, me. I was there.

I'm looking at myself watching him in the reflection. My young eyes are wide, my lips muttering something wordless, and I briefly flicker with the memory of that longing.

Bridge I breathed *you knew?* He was now somewhere to my left.

Well, yeah. We were young, you weren't subtle.

I watch myself pocket two dollars from the machine.

I was wearing skinny jeans that day, I remembered. I didn't have pockets.

// I can't believe you did that.

Me either.

// They were going out of business anyway. Too late, arcades were already done.

2010 Bridge smacks my butt when he wins.

//

Bridge's east coast Australian test server sat in an old mine, cooled underground in a filled-in open cut. I learned this when my obsession finally bubbled over — imagining myself up there on that stage, slowly blurring out of memory in a collective vision that Bridge got to curate. Seeing myself // in the eyes of onlookers at the arcade // as an unwelcome thief.

Bridge's product rolled out. His company got listed. He had a baby. I watch Bridge's little algorithm and his little gammin $589 headset take over the ancestry.com crowd // boomers who think of themselves as endlessly interesting meticulously documenting and reliving their newspaper routes. Mob, understandably deprived of collective archival resources, flock to it too — but are vastly outnumbered and outbought.

I showed ngaamba who // thrilled // began sharing her stories about her early life // about what it was like to be that girl waiting quietly in agony by the railway that cut the town in half with coal // waiting for me to burst out. She told me // and Bridge's little test server mic // what it was like for my father to limp her into the waiting room and into a chair // to be ignored until the last possible moment. To watch us later play *Super Street Fighter II* limp with jealous want. To curl her hair after a decade of crushing it. She told me more, she told Bridge's server even more.

I want some of this to be … secret while I'm around, okay?
I don't want no questions // You can look the rest when I'm
gone.

The way this memory is going means that you must know
that by 2032, after months of talking to a microphone,
my mother died. She went without peace // begging to be
removed from the hospital separated between our home and
the train line.

It's that separation I thought of on my way to Bridge's
servers.

//

It took a year before I finally sat with ngambaa's stories in
the headset Bridge gifted me all that time ago. I found the
geolocation. I found the calendar. What was she doing when
she was seventeen?

My mother's at the railway line at sunset, I see her clutching
her stomach with her fists. Her face is drained of colour, she
is grey and brown and green like a eucalypt. She whimpers,
too proud to make much noise, not that it would matter
while the coal train thunders on and with my father yelling
in the driver's seat.

The light shifts quick, though the sun does not yet set. Like a set of new myopic eyes. My mother, suddenly, has a generic composite in place of her face. Her wails are loud now, keening and undignified.

I see Bridge's mother. She is pregnant. She comes over to my mother, eases her out of the driver's seat. My mother, who would not even allow me to move her from bed to a shower in her final days, complies, opens her legs to this strange wadjin. She births me there, by a never-ending train and a nice white woman with a big farmstead, until I'm out, bloody and squashed.

Bridge's mum clutches me against her stomach. She bounces me lovingly up and down. My mother laughs. It's a sound totally unfamiliar to me. A titter, from a profoundly serious woman. My mother pinches this woman's face and breathes *Thank you, thank you, thank you.*

// There was some loud rumble coming deep from in my ears. // Beneath it, my pulse hissed in a quick rhythm that I didn't feel in my chest as much as it was surging through the nape of my neck. I knew immediately. *That dead dying dog cunt!* // I'm blurring out on his school stage. I'm impossibly pocketing two stolen dollars at his arcade. I'm looking through the white gaze of that bitch who watched the Cronulla riots and offered me KFC.

Bridge left me with this, this algorithmic composite of his own damn fantasies, absolute ngurragah bastardisation of —

I paused. *No. Surely he wouldn't have the fucking nerve.*

//

It's a long time ago. A gruff white man with a rifle weaves his way through tall grasses and short trees. He has a pregnant wadjin in tow. She has the same effortless straight hair as Bridge and his mother, the same pinched flushed cheeks. She knots her dress above her knee.

I wait for what I know happens on Bridge's little family homestead here, but it doesn't yet come.

I watch this blanking-out scene for hours — when will it

happen? I'm observing the rifle like I observed Bridge's hands in *Super Street Fighter II*. My eyes flicker to his great great grandfather's face, like I did to Bridge in the glass of the 1993 classic.

Do it, you dog I grind through my teeth. *I know you're about to.*

But he doesn't. ████████████████████████
████████████████████████████████
████████████████████████████████
████████████████████████████████
██████████████████

He ████████████ He ██████████████████
████████████████████████████████
████████████████████████████████
██████████████

He takes the baby, and the rifle, and ██████████████
██████████████

I take my hand through my braid reflexively. *Lots of stories* Bridge had hedged in 2026. *As it really happened.*

//

It's a cold night when I got to the east coast test servers. I traced that coal train line up to where I guessed they'd be housed, if the mine was an old coal one from 1993. The guards, paid shit all on gig apps anyway, weren't hard at all to bribe even from a skinny jean pocket. I turned up with two jerry cans — they must have known someone would eventually.

It was unceremonious. I made a quick apology to my mother, whose memories // in whatever form they were now // I would be destroying with the rest. I poured petrol down the cooling shafts. I patted my pockets // I tried to think of something definitive to say. I could barely catalogue in my own mind the wrongs // imagining Bridge's beautiful armpits, his gleeful face, his forceful grasp. The dying dog cunt.

The moment for my triumph passed. I just stood there, as limp dicked and covered in sweat as I was the night I failed to fuck Bridge into a pillow. I lowered // my face to peer into the shafts // somewhere below I // could see a green flicker light // a heartbeat.

You'll blow yourself up if you light it like that! // The guard hollered from his post.

He was right. I lay face down // watching ngambaa's // little heartbeat // among the shadow of Bridge's wires // until I couldn't anymore. I know it's pathetic. I think of Bridge's foot on my chest // *You know, that's not how this is gonna work.*

I picked up the empty cans. I've got another two hundred in here somewhere. *Hey dhagaan, could you, like when I'm away // could you do it for me? It's already in there, I just —*

He said // *Sure, man. Won't be able to buy one of them headsets for years anyway.*

I watched the conflagration from a hill.

//

Bridge's business was barely impacted. But eventually // I guess // he figures it out or the guard blabs to get a free headset // because in 2034 Bridge was at my doorstep.

Those thick hands immediately gripped at my face. He's tugging at my eyelids, shaking my head back and forth, grunting without words. High punch, low punch, high punch high punch high punch. I crumpled. Low punch low punch low punch.

I was prone on the ground, legs splayed, when he just hardened his jaw and looked at me intently, as if he were memorising me. Bridge reaches behind him and produces a Version 4 headset // which he threw at my stomach. I retched.

He left me then, he was gasping, I was grasping that headset. In the memory Bridge reaches gingerly up to kiss me, that night in 2014. He whispers — *Thank you thank you thank you.* I glitch a little // and

// then I spit on his face again and again and again and again and again and again and again.

Guyuggwa

LANIYUK

The pulse of drums and dancing feet echoed across the night's air. Calls and laughter grasped the wind, dancing through the Maunga, already heavily laden with summer's gifts. The return of fresh air, after weeks of smoke, ash and rubble, nurtured a sigh of relief into Guyuggwa's hardened brow. Pressed between bodies, the glow of the bonfire swelled as more debris was added, casting shadows across tired faces, streaked with the dreaming tears of relief.

Ahi caught their eye and reached for their hand, stroking the flesh of their calloused palm, gesturing for them to leave. They'd both been working in Resources for the past couple of years after being reallocated from the front line. Once farm land had been seized the re-distribution of goods and medicine became the primary goal. With the collapse of the Common Wealth and the successful coup d'état, the constant violence had simmered and their work on the front line had been less pressing. Māori had been slowly shifting attention from seizing back their Ancestral Wealth to coordinating the coming change. In some rare moments, while pressed between bodies and swaying in the back of a truck during drop offs, sometimes, Ahi even felt at peace.

The remains of a crumbling city smiled down at them as they slid through the crowds. A cluster of teens held each other, hugging waists, sweat dripping down their necks as they sang, jumping higher and higher. Ahi quickly calculated a short cut and took a sharp right after the group, griping Guyuggwa's hand and pulling them towards the Maunga. That night the Elders had announced that the time of war was finally over. Tomorrow we would begin anew. Aotearoa had erupted with celebrations across both islands as The People marked the end of tyranny and control. A spark, centuries in the making, touched the final strong holds of white supremacy and imperial rule covering the evenings celebrations in a beautiful warm flame. Shadows danced across the faces of a people, born between earth and war.

Slipping into quieter streets, Ahi and Guyuggwa walked hand in hand. The glow and heat of bodies cooled into a soft summer slumber as they stalled in front of a mound of rubble and dirt, lingering.

'Remember when this was a supermarket Ahi? They sold kūmara at triple its value.'

'Yeah ... they also sold the best chocolate. Fuck, I miss chocolate.'

Guyuggwa chuckled. 'I don't miss our birthright to food being withheld from us. Like we didn't deserve to eat.'

Ahi swallowed a laugh and dramatically threw their arms in the air. 'Yeah ... But fuck! That hazelnut chocolate! Remember when we stole a block and ate it down at the beach? We had to take three blankets, it was that fucking cold.'

Guyuggwa nodded slowly with a smile, looking beyond the pile of dust and dirt.

'That was right before we seized control of the highways. Remember that mission out to the west coast?'

Ahi turned away from the boulders of cement and rotting wood. 'We lost Daniel that day.'

'And Mornah.'

'Yeah ... and Mornah.'

The air had stilled as they walked down the residential streets. Guyuggwa side stepped a young Kawakawa plant, pushing through the concrete, cracking cement, unfurled and bouyant in the softness of the evening. Some of these streets hadn't seen a car in years. The Common Wealth had cut Aotearoa off from international trade but with the urban farms taking off and local infrastructure meeting most of the needs of people within the area, fuel had been saved for the most urgent transport and for now, that was enough.

Guyuggwa took a moment to peer into the houses whose doors were swung open, fires blazing in the backyards, children running through the streets, laughing and singing in their sovereign tongue. A newborn slept in the lap of a nanna sitting on a nearby porch. She smiled and nodded as they slowly walked past, returning the smile.

'Can you believe it, Guyuggwa. That baby will never know life living in the colony, will always know their language, will always practise culture. Imagine what that generation will be capable of, imagine what they'll create and who they'll be.'

'I can't even begin to,' Guyuggwa whispered. 'It's taken us so long to get here. I don't even know who I am outside of struggle.' Guyuggwa's voice caught in their throat as they tilted their chin to the night's sky, thick with smoke and ash. They hadn't seen the stars in months. 'I've spent my whole life fighting and resisting. How am I supposed to raise up children when I've spent so long pushing back the colony?'

Thick tears rolled down their cheeks. 'I don't know softness, I don't know healing. I know building myself up after they tore me down. I know building muscle and growing scars to soften the next blow. I've forgotten who I am before all of this.'

Ahi nodded, more to themselves, feeling inside their chest for something of their own, not thrusted upon them by the colony. Following Guyuggwa's gaze into the night sky they rolled their shoulders back for the first time in nearly 400 years.

'I just—' Guyuggwa bit their lower lip and swallowed slowly, allowing the tears to fall where they landed, closing their eyes to the sting and itch of smoke. 'I'm just so broken.'

There was nothing to see in the sky, no distinct shapes or lights, just the clotted blanket of the colony burning.

Ahi reached for Guyuggwa's hand, blinking into the darkness, tears pricking at the corners of their eyes and swallowed hard. Taking a deep breathe, they promised the night's sky and every heart that had beat since The Beginning:

'We're not broken.'

Resting their forehead on Guyuggwa's shoulder they watched their own tears fall into their woven fingers.

'We're not broken. We deserved better than this. We deserved safety, we deserved Language, we deserved a home on our homelands. We were denied that and we did the best that we could with what we had. Things are different now, we have control over our futures and can make better choices than the people before us.'

Guyuggwa had arrived nearly a decade earlier from a posting in the Eora Nations. Warriors and strategists had been sent over to support the Māori Resistance when the Common Wealth had doubled down, re-seizing Pasifika lands and closing off the Ancestral trade routes. It had been nearly twenty years since leaving their Sovereign Lands in the north. Two decades since the Larrakia salt water had tasted the sweat and melanin of their skin. It wasn't the sounds of one hundred people sleeping in a dorm that kept them up, but the stone sitting in their stomach that churned, telling them their lands had forgotten them. Five years into their posting the crown broke through the north west, claiming Yawuru land. Cross ocean travel had been difficult while so many resources were pushed to where they were needed the most. Since the empire had fallen, Elders everywhere were calling people home. Ceremony was required, loved ones needed to Tjalak and Country needed to be healed.

Tomorrow they would be announcing the boats that would be taking people to the Eora Nations, from there it would be weeks of travel inland and north before they finally returned.

A returning to their Sovereign Lands but this time, not as an unwilling subject of the british empire, not as a pawn to white supremacy, but with the heavy feet of the Larrakia people. Not heavy with the weight and burden of settler colonialism but with the abundance of their Sovereign Inheritance. Laden with the songs of their ancestors and the dancing of their descendants. The first time in four centuries they would arrive a free people.

Guyuggwa's Nardang had been leading the rehousing program when they left all those years ago, but since their Nardla's passing during a raid, they weren't so sure where their family was. The Nimeybirra that were knee high when they left would be adults now. Everything was different.

Boots hit concrete as they scaled the stairs. Perilously close to the edge of the sloping hill, its rotten railing had given way long before people had been relocated after the bombings. Guyuggwa kicked their shoes off at the door, dropped their socks on the floor and collapsed on the mattress. It had been nearly three days since they'd slept more than two hours, the anticipation of freedom too powerful to sleep through. Ahi gently closed the door behind them as they entered the room. They were certain that the other Warriors were still out enjoying the celebration, but something about the slowly blooming morning light called for the gentleness.

Sliding in next to Guyuggwa, they tucked their brown curls behind their ears and kissed the top of their forehead, pulling them in closer. Depending on what the Elders were going to prioritise, the boats would probably leave for The Eora anywhere from a couple of weeks to a few months and Guyuggwa would be on the first round of boats. There hadn't been a conversation about what would happen between them once the colony was overthrown. They both knew what would happen.

'What's the first thing you're gonna do when you get home?'

Guyuggwa tossed the sheets over them and rested further into the arch of Ahi's body, gazing through the window, watching the first light kiss the tree tops and ocean.

'After seeing my Alap, obviously.'

'Obviously!' chimed Ahi, leaning their head into the curve of Guyuggwa's neck and watching the sky blush soft pink.

'I'm gonna go to the beach and jump straight into that water. It's gonna be hot, it's gonna be humid and I'll finally be home.'

The ocean wind exhaled over the Maunga, gently pushing the thicker layers of smoke aside. Guyuggwa and Ahi held each other and watched the last of the colony burn to the ground, ash rising to the skies.

Tea

FLORA CHOL

The process
that is tea
is the convention
that transcribes
the memories
the stories
we lock up
for so long
& throw away
the key to

My memory in tea
is bittersweet
solace taking me back
to the days
in Khartoum when
peanut butter salad
was the best thing
in the world

When a hot
afternoon perched beneath
the parched shade
of the Masket
tree while
watching our mama
stitch flowers on
bedsheets
was the best day
in the world

When being a
little girl on
Christmas day was
the best day
in the world

Taking me back
to the time
when our mama
went away for
a long time
our aunty dressed
us all up
in our Sunday
best on Christmas
day to see
our mama far away

Taking me back
to the best
day in the world
when cousin Suzanna
& I wore
our Sunday best on
Christmas day

Matching dresses
red & white
with lace hems
& mini stars
all over
Aunty said we
looked like angels

Suzanna was the Angel
this was the
best day in
the world
the day that
Suzanna died was
the worst day
in the world.

Alt-Dream

MERRYANA SALEM

Three things happened when the government gave you your Deadline: you got a tonne of condolence junk mail, your bank accounts closed, and within a month, law expected you to turn up to a hospital to die. So, as she sipped her fourth cup of tea with her cat in her lap, Thea Jonas was surprised to get notifications for charges to her bank account from ALT-DREAM INC.

Thea's eye twitched, as she scanned the list of random withdrawals. Had the Bank warned her of closing account fees?

12:01AM	ALT-DREAM INC.	$6.07
12:02AM	ALT-DREAM INC.	$2.97
12:03AM	ALT-DREAM INC.	$20.09

Her phone buzzed, jerking Thea out of her reverie; splashing her tea down her front and dislodging Peanut. Her mum's dimples flashed for a few seconds, and Thea slid the photo up to answer.

'Are you ignoring your mother? I called five times. Five! Were you with that Leila?'

'I have a month, Mum.'

'So?'

'So, spending my final days with the woman who 'just wants to be friends' is not on the bucket list.'

The faux indignation faded from her mother's voice, 'I just wanted to check you hadn't— '

'I won't change my Deadline, Mum — promise.' Thea sighed. 'Mum, the bank didn't contact you, did they? Got these gammon charges to my account.'

'Call 'em.'

'Yeah, I will,' Thea lied. The certainty of her death had not alleviated her phone anxiety.

'Also,' her mum hesitated. 'You know the painting I gave you, the Women's Business one?'

Thea eyed the interconnecting pink and yellow dots swirling in the painting above her couch, beaming shiny in the morning light. 'Yeah?'

'Don't—' Her mother's deep breath rattled the connection. 'Don't give it to anyone, okay? It's yours, but when you go-' she swallowed hard.

'Course, Mum. Only if you take Peanut.'

Her mum's cackle sounded choked, 'That bloody cat hates me.'

'She hates you with love!' Thea laughed. They both did,

and it was almost like before. 'Anyway Mum, I gotta make some calls. Message you later?'

'Bye, bub. Love you.'

Peanut had returned to Thea's lap, only to be dethroned when Thea rolled off her bean bag onto the floor. She lay there, staring up at the flickering shadows on the ceiling cast by passing cars below the window.

The smell of pizza grease wafted through the window from the tuckshop below, combining with the soggy boxes stacked a few feet away in the kitchen. Only 30 days left of this, she thought. Of late-night takeaways, four cups of tea before 9am mornings, the tickle of Peanut's whiskers as she investigated why she was on the floor. Ancient lint matted into the rug pressed into her palms as she pushed herself upright.

Shaking her curls from her eyes, Thea retrieved her laptop from the couch, and slumped into the middle cushion. Her laptop gurgled on. After a minute she was logging into the Bank. Thea resolved to do what anyone under 30 with debilitating phone anxiety would. Either resolve it online, or resign herself to the issue for the rest of her days, which, luckily, weren't many.

After a moan from her laptop's innards, the sole inhabitants of her wiped account appeared. Thea pushed aside an impulse to text Leila. Instead, she hovered the cursor over the first transaction, frowning. Unlike on her phone, ALT-DREAM INC. flashed hyperlink blue.

Shrugging, she clicked the link.

A webpage with a worn green background and a grey bar opened. Above the bar, shiny black font read:

WELCOME TO ALT-DREAM.
ENTER YOUR CODE

Thea dragged a hand down her face, and crossed her legs. What code? She searched her email for anything ALT-DREAM. A slew of correspondence from fast fashion stores she'd bought from over the last ten years greeted her efforts, all of them offering Deadline discounts alongside automated Condolences. Rolling her eyes, she checked her messages, glancing at the last meme Leila sent her, and finding a lot of nothing about a code. ALT-DREAM'S only correspondence? Charging non-existent money.

A search, correcting her and directing to the ultra-stream, was equally fruitless. Thea tasted apple from her shampoo as she chewed on the ends of her hair. Maybe Leila had heard of ALT-DREAM. Someone else must have. Or were the amounts too random? Thea reopened the transaction list.

'Not to brag, Pea, but I could've been a genius!'

Peanut didn't look up from cleaning her ginger bum at the exclamation. Thea copied the 7 amounts into ALT-DREAM'S code bar. After deleting the points between the numbers, a code consisting of 26 numbers filled the grey box, and she hit enter.

A large green tick occupied the screen, then another screen loaded. This time, three blank boxes asked her to confirm her full name, Deadline, and race. With her eyes practically shut, Thea typed: Thea Cynthia Jonas, 20th November 2029, Gringai. No sooner had she finished than a message appeared.

WELCOME TO ALT-DREAM, THEA.

AFTER THE ESTABLISHMENT OF DEADLINES IN 2025 FOR POPULATION CONTROL, ALT-DREAM IS DEDICATED TO PROVIDING DEADLINERS COMFORT FROM UNCERTAINTY VIA AN IMMERSIVE STREAMING EXPERIENCE.

ALT-DREAM PROVIDES UNLIMITED VIEWING OF YOUR POSSIBILITIES FOR ALLEVIATION, ENTERTAINMENT, AND CURIOSITY UNTIL THE DAY OF YOUR DEADLINE FOR FREE.

BY CLICKING AGREE, YOU AGREE TO NOT SHARE, SPEAK, PUBLISH, OR COMMUNICATE ABOUT ALT-DREAM IN ANY FORM.

ALT-DREAM WILL KNOW.
OUR CONDOLENCES.

*ONCE YOU CLOSE ALT-DREAM, IT CANNOT BE ACCESSED

ALT-DREAM INC.

Clicking Agree could be tricky advertising to lure her into a scheme. There were stories about Deadliners falling for them. But unless ALT-DREAM was desperate to hear Leila's drunken flirty voice recordings, or see the photos of her great grandparents marrying on Country, she had nothing worth stealing. With an apprehension usually reserved for calls, Thea agreed.

The screen went black, and those cups of tea hammered her bladder. For a few horribly infinite moments, there was nothing but ringing in Thea's ears and the yawn of her laptop fan.

Finally. An interface not dissimilar to Youtube loaded; with a box clearly reserved for video occupying the top half, and SUGGESTED STREAMS tiled beneath. Thea exhaled, examining the tiles under the space. One was labelled, 'Entertainment Course', another 'Ballet Pursuit', and another 'Luke Chamber'.

All the moisture evaporated from Thea's throat. Luke was the only white boy she'd ever dated. At nineteen, unable to reconcile being Blak with liking women, she'd figured queer Blak women couldn't exist. Meanwhile, Luke was the first boy that hadn't shrunk away from her, or made her feel small. It had been a crush held by hope of a cure from self-hate. It didn't last. Why would it? But why was his name here?

She shook her head and kept scrolling. She ground her teeth as she read the suggestions that flicked across, until one labelled 'No Social Feed' caught her eye. She clicked it.

It took a moment to recognise her apartment. There was no purple couch, in its place a single green armchair, and the brick wall behind was the crumbling coffee-stain brown it had been when she moved in. But the window was the same, minus abandoned half-drunk tea mugs. A woman staggered into frame with a crew cut, and red lipstick smeared up her cheek. Thea squinted, spotting empty bottles and an overflowing ashtray by the chair. With a belch the stranger collapsed, hopefully asleep, into the armchair.

The video had a progress bar. Thea wiped the sweat from her palms on her jeans, before clicking an earlier point in the timeline. The image pixelated, before sputtering, settling on her mother, carrying Women's Business from the apartment. Face red, eyes bloodshot, her mum put the frame down to wipe her nose on her sleeve as a date flashed in the stream's top right corner: 20/11/24

Thea clapped a hand over mouth. Years ago — 2024, she supposed — she had thought quitting all her social feeds would ease her mental health. She'd even messaged Leila, bragging of the grand idea.

Sixty minutes later, Leila had barged into the apartment with ice cream, devon rolls, and a slide presentation titled 'Isolating Yourself When You're Clinically Lonely? Shut Ya Hole'. Over the next few days, she kept Thea from her habit of taking a dish scourer to her thighs. She even drove Thea to her first psychiatrist. Thea had decided not to think about the alternative to Leila's staying then, but ALT-DREAM had.

Believing in the multiverse was one thing, providing it as deathbed entertainment was another. Hell, they had 4K vision of it. Thea pulled out her phone; searching for any recent major discoveries relating to multiverse and surveillance. The results revolved mostly around 80s B-Grade sci-fi novels, and a video series with 200 views titled 'THE MULTIVERSE EXPLAINS SMALLPOX' by a balding white man with the username 'vaxxthevaxxers'.

Outside, the weather had turned. The grey window matched the now dulled grey of the ceiling. Thea walked over to it and threw it open. Exhaust, pizza grease, and garlic drifted on the air with the horns and shouts. Somewhere, someone was blaring the Macarena through aging speakers. Thea rested her chin against folded elbows on the sill. After a moment, Peanut jumped up to sit beside her, blinking slowly up at her. Thea breathed in, counted to five and exhaled.

Grabbing her phone, Thea dialled Leila. It was warm from being in her pocket, a pleasant contrast to the coolness of the breeze. Leila picked up on the third ring.

'Thee?'

Thea's heart jumped toward her brain. 'Hellooooo,' she managed.

Leila laughed in a rhythmic mumble, 'What are you doing?'

'I wanted to ask you,' Thea inhaled, 'about the multiverse?'

'Uh … any particular reason?' Bottles clinked behind her

voice with a shout for a Tooheys.

Thea pulled at her hair. 'Just watching something.'

The clatter of glass clinking on wood before she answered. 'Any good?'

Thea hesitated, pushing herself away from the sill to begin pacing around the coffee table.

'Thee?'

'Do you think ... do you think you saved my life?'

'What?'

'A few years ago, we'd just met, and I was gonna go off Socials.'

Leila cackled, but Thea heard a door close. 'Oh, yeah. Not your most brilliant idea. Lucky, you listen to me occasionally.'

'Lucky,' muttered Thea.

'So, now you're wondering if there's a universe where you listen to me more?' Her voice echoed. She must have ducked into the toilet.

Thea rested her forehead in her hand. 'More like wondering, if you think I only— ' she threw herself back down onto the couch. 'Do you think I only love you because you saved me?'

Silence, the kind that crawled under Thea's nails. She checked her phone screen. The call was still active. Thea began chewing her pinky nail. 'Because,' she yanked the word from her mouth with the finger, 'it was before that.'

'Thea— '

'When we met at Blak faculty trivia night, remember? You were wearing those jeans with scribbles of eyes? You said you drew them on, stained with bleach, or something- I thought they looked cool, but I didn't want to ask how you did it. So, next day, after you left my apartment, I tried bleaching my jeans. They dissolved in the machine. Mucked spectacularly. But everytime I smell bleach, or see an eye, I think of how you were the only person on our trivia team that could recite the Patterson poem that won us the bonus round. Because fuck Australiana, you told me, but the rhymes are a pretty distraction.' Thea rubbed her face with the back of her hand. 'I just— I just need you to know it was you then. From then, and now.'

'Your Deadline is next month, Thea. You're dying next month. You think those gubbas at Deadline make exceptions for gay Blak women?'

'No. But a month can be a ways away.'

'I have to go.'

'Leila-?'

'I know.'

The line clicked quiet and Thea hurled her phone across the room. It hit the floor with a thud that sent Peanut flying, yelping as she leapt off the window sill, and knocking Thea's coolamon from its place on the couch arm as she flew for the bedroom. Puffing out her cheeks, Thea smushed her face into the nearest pillow and allowed herself a single scream.

ALT-DREAM was waiting. Thea imagined steam pouring from her ears as she returned to her laptop. The pale woman was still slumped in her green chair in Thea's apartment, mouth hanging open for a few faint snores to escape. Thea scrolled further through the suggested streams. Some were labelled in French, Arabic, one was even in Latin, but Thea needed something more distracting than what her life might have looked like had she stayed in the Latin course she dropped in the third week of uni.

Other streams boasted names of people she vaguely remembered from holidays, classes, clubs. One was named for a town she'd been offered a job in just because she was Aboriginal, and they'd assumed she spoke the language of a place 1000 kilometres from home. Thea kept scrolling, reading names and places until she remembered and forgot them all over again. Peanut was whining for a treat with the distinctive scratching pops of her kneading the rug, but a thumbnail finally stopped Thea's search. Gringai. The tips of her fingers tingled as she clicked the stream and made it full-screen.

Her own face stared back at her, warm light brown under a mop of indecisive wavy curls, and lit by her computer. Thea couldn't help but glance up. Yep. Her octopus sticker was still covering the webcam. This Thea was not her. Well, she was. Could have been.

Three buzzes. Thea plunged a hand into her pocket, but her phone was still. Instead Other Thea stood and walked out of the frame. The date in the video's corner flashed today's. Another today.

'Helloooo?' Other Thea answered out of view. 'How's work?' Thea pressed her ear to her crackling laptop speaker, as if this would allow her to hear the other end of a phone line in another universe. 'Oh, okay,' Other Thea agreed with the person calling. It was no good. Thea lifted her head and felt her eyebrows scrunch together.

The painting. Her mum's art. It wasn't there. Where her mother's art had been in every other stream that Thea skimmed, there was only the pixelated impression of faded white paint over brick. Thea full-screened the feed, zooming in. Missing too, from where Peanut regularly pushed it to the floor in protest, was the coolamon she'd carved with Pop. She'd kept it since she was six. Since her Pop had taught her their mob. But not this Thea.

She was wrapping up the call, 'Don't rush home, babe. It's not like I'm a Deadliner. We have time.'

In every other universe Thea saw, she and her family were proud. Messy, loud, a little late realising it, but Blak with art and anger. Anger that it took until Thea was six for her Pop to confess he wasn't Spanish. But not this Other Thea. In every other universe, Thea had a Deadline. But not in this one. Thea tasted blood from her nail as Other Thea ran to get a knock at the door.

'I told you no rush,' Other Thea giggled.

'I couldn't wait to see you,' the pale woman from 'No

Social Feed' twirled Other Thea into the frame, kissing her as they stumbled, laughing. 'Finally call your mum, today?'

Other Thea grimaced, her hands around the other woman's waist. 'No. What would we even talk about?'

Salt mixed with the metallic taste in Thea's mouth. On the fourth try, her shaking hand managed to hit pause. With her head cocked to the side, Peanut eyed her from beside the face down coolamon. Thea stumbled to her feet, stooping to scratch Peanut's ears and pick up the coolamon. Once she'd restored it to the arm of the couch, Thea rubbed her eyes. Fur from Peanut stuck to her cheeks as she did. Thea counted the ginger hairs as she pulled them off her damp face, and focused on breathing. When her breath finally slowed, the clouds outside had thickened pink in the dusk. Beneath the pink was the dull frustrated hum of peak hour. Thea emptied some biscuits into Peanut's bowl, messaged her mum to see if she was home safe, inspected the inside of her empty fridge, and stayed on her feet.

Ignoring the growl from her stomach, Thea downed four glasses of water then another two, after she peed. Now squatting on the floor, she stared up at Women's Business above the couch until each hitch in the dots, the shein of the black, the stray cat hairs floating in the last of the daylight blurred together. Her gaze dropped back to her laptop on the floor.

What else could ALT-DREAM know of her life to show her what she hadn't lived? The question lodged in her throat, in the shadows cast on the bricks, in the smell of the garbage she'd yet to throw away. Maybe she'd already done it elsewhere. Maybe it was the difference between her and dying.

Chin resting on her knees, Thea's hand was lingering on play, when the sound of a set of keys shaking in her lock made her jump. She had barely twisted her neck to look around when the scent of pine wood, disinfectant, and booze announced Leila's entrance.

Blinking up at her, Thea closed her dropped jaw as Leila threw her bags onto the couch and crouched beside Thea. Their faces were so close, she could see a smattering of new freckles above Leila's immaculately bushy eyebrows.

'You better haunt me for this, Thee.'

'Me and your aunties gotta find something to do while you take your sweet time.'

Without taking her eyes off Thea's lips, Leila's hand snapped Thea's laptop lid shut, tilted her chin up until their gaze met, and kissed her.

እኔ ሃገር የለኝም

ይርጋ ገላው ወልደየስ

ከእኔን መሳይ አፈር - እንዳሳረፍሁ እግሬን፤
'ከየት መጣህ?' ብሎ ጠየቀኝ ሃገሬን።

እጆቸን አነሳሁ ወደሰማዩ ጥግ፤
ተመልከተው አልሁት- የድንቅነሽ አጥንት፤
በዳሎል እንፉሎት፤
በአባይ ውሀ ትነት ፤
ወደሰማይ ሲያርግ።።

ተመልከት ሰማይ ላይ ከበሮ ሲመታ፤
በነጎድጓድ ጮኽት በመብረቅ ብልጭታ፤
የጥንቶቸ መንፈስ ተጠርተው በሆታ፤
ወደ ምድር ሲፈሱ ከቆምሁበት ቦታ፤
ሃገራቸው ሲሆን የልቤ ትርታ።።

ሃገሩ ወዴት ነው ብለህ አትጠይቀኝ፤
በሰማይ በምድር በግራና በቀኝ፤
የኔ የማይለኝ የለም የማያውቀኝ።።

I have no country

YIRGA GELAW WOLDEYES

As I rest my feet on the soil that looks like me
He asks, 'Where is your country?'
I raise my hands to the corner of the sky.
I say, Look:
On the vapours of Dallol
And the mists of Abay
The bones of Dinknesh
Are ascending.
Drums beat in the clouds
Rumbling thunder, lightning songs
The spirits of the ancients gather
Pour down on the soil at my feet
Making my heartbeat their country.

Do not ask me where my country is.
On the left and on the right,
In heaven and on earth
There is no one who does not know me.

ማዶ ላሊበላ ወዲህም ኡሉሩ፤
ህልምና ቃልኪዳን አለምን ሲፈጥሩ፤
አስር ፕላኔቶች ከአለት የወቀሩ፤
ከአጥንቴ ላይ ቆመው በደሜ 'ሚዞሩ፤
ሰላም፤ ካያ፤ እያሉ፤
አሁን እዚህ አሉ።

የዋጉል ስጦታ ያ ደርባን ያርጋን፤
'በድንበር ካፈኑት ሃገር ምን ያደርጋን?'
ብሎ ውቅያኖስ ሆድ ከአባይ ጋር ያወጋ።

ኮኮብ ነው ጫማዋ ብርሃን ነው ልብሴ፤
ቀስተደመና ነው ፈገግ ሲል ጥርሴ፤
እኔ ሃገር የለኝም ሃገር ነኝ ራሴ።

ከምታየው ሁሉ ከሚርመሰመሰው፤
በህዋው ገላ ውስጥ ሞልቶ ከፈሰሰው፤
ቢታደል አያልቅም አንድ አለም ላንድ ሰው።

የግጥሜን ጉባኤ ተመልከት ጨረቃ፤
በእልፍ ታዳሚዎች ሞልታ ተጥለቅልቃ፤
በአበቦች ብርሃን መድረኩን አድምቃ፤
በጉጉት ስታየኝ መምጣቴን ጠብቃ።

There Lalibela, here Uluru
Covenant and Dreaming created the world.
They who carved ten planets from a rock
Stand in my bones, run in my veins
Selam, Kaya
They are saying now.

There, in the womb of the ocean
The gift of the Wagul
Great river Derbarl Yerrigan
Meets with Abay, saying,
'What worth is a country when stifled by borders?'

Stars are my shoes, light is my cloth
My teeth, in smile, are a rainbow.
I do not have a country,
I am a country myself.

The abundance you see
Overflowing the body of the universe
Is greater than if every person took one world.

Look at the moon, the conference of my poems
Filled with tens of thousands of listeners
Lighting the stage with glowing flowers
Yearning for my arrival.

በቋንቋና በእውቀት በዘላለም ኑሮ፤
ገደብ የለበትም የነፍሴ ተፈጥሮ።
ነፍስ ነው አካሌ የልጅነት መዝሙር፤
ከእሳት በላይ ውሃ ከውሃ በላይ ምድር፤
አነባብሮ ይዞ ህዋውን የሚዞር።

የጸሃይን መስኮት ከፍቶ የሚዘጋ፤
የብርሃን እግሮች አጥፎ እሚዘረጋ፤
ነፍስ ነው ትንፍሼ ተራራ 'ሚወጋ፤
ውሃ ነው መንፈሴ እሳት ላይ የረጋ፤
ህይወት የሚያበቅል ካፈር ሲዘረጋ።

በተጻፈ ታሪክ መኖር ነው ባርነት፤
አለመታጠር ነው ትርጉሙ ነጻነት።
መሬት ነው አካሌ ሰማዩ ነው ነፍሴ፤
እኔ ሃገር የለኝም ሃገር ነኝ ራሴ።

In language, in knowledge, in eternal life
The essence of my soul is boundless
The wind is my body, songs of childhood
Water above fire, earth above water
Holding it together, moving in space.

Opening and closing the windows of the sun
Folding and stretching the legs of light
My breath is a wind that pierces mountains
My spirit is water that sleeps on fire
Life grows up, when I lie down on sand.

Slavery is to live by a written history,
Freedom is to be unbounded.
Earth is my body
Sky is my soul
I do not have a country,
I am country myself.

The poem reflects on that question often asked to Black people: 'Where is your country?' So often, this is not a genuine question, but one that seeks to decentre us from the place where we live and call home. Additionally, so often the answer is already assumed, that we must come from some place of suffering. This poem uses Indigenous Ethiopian and Australian philosophy on existence and place to turn this question on its head, to say that my heritage makes me a country beyond what the questioner can understand. The poem presents the essence of being human as an embodiment of spirit and nature. Life is constituted by boundless things that extend to infinite time and space. This decentres the belief in being a citizen of one country. It also speculates on how black people can gain freedom by being 'unbounded', by refusing to be tied to the written histories and accounts of who they are.

In Ethiopian Indigenous philosophy, human beings have seven forces that belong to the body and the soul. The body is created from four natural forces: wind, fire, water, and soil. The soul is made of three forces: language, knowledge, and immortality or eternal life. It is also believed that the world is constituted by the four forces of the body: the soil which lies on water, the water on fire, and the fire on wind (wind is the core, holding everything). Wind is also associated with childhood, with children seen to embody wind. As people age, they are aligned with other elements, from fire through to water and finally to soil.

The poem uses Indigenous names of places and rivers. Instead of the Swan River, it uses Derbarl Yerrigan. Abay is the Ethiopian name for the Nile. Dallol is a volcanic place in Ethiopia, famous for having the highest average temperatures on record on Earth. Dinknesh is the Ethiopian name for 'Lucy', one of the oldest skeletal remains of human ancestors ever found in the world. Ethiopia and Australia are linked through sacred places like Lalibela and Uluru, and the ancestors of these places live in the poet's veins, speaking words of welcome and peace in Amharic and Noongar (*Selam, Kaya*).

The translation is as close to the original Amharic as possible, but with major phrasing changes given English and Amharic have such different syntax structures. Unfortunately, the English translation loses much of the Amharic rhyme and rhythm, but I have tried to make the English as elegant as possible while still communicating the Amharic message.

Thylacine

JASPER WYLD

Ever since I was a young girl, there has been talk of bringing the Thylacine back to life.

Headlines pop up now and again, separated only by a few years. They're always the same. Scientists, they claim, could use the DNA of a Thylacine to bring them back from the depths of extinction. Here, the articles always show the same photo of that jar containing a preserved joey. Its lifeless body is without any fur and the wrinkles in its pale, old flesh are deep. The theory is that a cloned Thylacine embryo can be made to gestate in an extant marsupial, a living breathing animal that would birth the past into the present.

Between these sporadic and stagnant articles are so-called sightings.

There have always been people, ever since the Thylacines died out in the 1930s, that claim there are others still out there, survivors in the wild. The most evidence these people ever produce, however, is a blurry video of an animal on the horizon, or a shaky recollection of an unusual howl in the night. Nevertheless, these stories find their way to the media and for a brief time a large question mark hangs over the Thylacine's extinction.

These articles — about the potential of cloning or claims of a new sighting — used to bring me hope, they used to excite me. When I was young, I fantasised about coming across a living Thylacine myself or at least one day witnessing their rebirth.

I grew out of this, of course.

With age came scepticism. Why was it that the media published these same articles over and over? Why was it that scientists claimed they could bring the Thylacine back, but never actually did it? Why were sightings never confirmed, never concrete?

I think I know the answer now and it has to do with the fact that almost all the people involved — from the scientists to the sighters, and the journalists that report on both — are whitefellas. What do whitefellas have to gain from the return of the Thylacine? No, not even that, what do they have to gain from the idea of its return, the story?

Because that's what these are. Stories. And they are the same story, when you get right down to it. They serve the same purpose. Fanciful talk of cloning, of reversing the Thylacine's demise, destabilises the unbreachable wall between extinct and extant, between the past and the present, death and life. These articles keep the door open, they suggest that history is not quite settled, that — if they chose to — they could go back and snatch the Thylacine from the grips of extinction. Sightings tell the same story. They suggest that the Thylacine never went extinct at all. They're still out there. We might not know where, we might not have proof, we might never have proof, but they're still out there and so what's the big deal? Murder isn't murder if there isn't a body, right?

These stories alleviate guilt, that's their true purpose. By throwing doubt onto the Thylacine's status as an extinct species, or by building hope that its extinction can be reversed, they are dodging responsibility for the sins inherited from their ancestors, the people who methodically extinguished this beautiful animal.

For make no mistake, invasion is what killed the Thylacine. They are a victim of colonialism, same as us. Bounties were placed on their heads, and for what? There is no proof that Thylacines were a threat to the wool industry. The farmers were failing and needed a scapegoat, a way to shirk responsibility, same as what's being done today.

And even now, during this time of mass extinction, with all the marsupials still alive under serious threat — going the way of the Thylacine so to speak — I still see the same damn articles.

ßWell, it looks like the scientists weren't bullshitting this time.

Government-funded research has finally turned all those ideas into reality. I just finished watching a livestream, along with a few hundred thousand others, of the Thylacine's rebirth. It was even more heart-wrenching than when I saw the only surviving footage of the Thylacine for the first time.

These last few months, the cloning of the Thylacine has dominated the news. Unlike the previous articles, these ones have substance. A fortnight ago the first ultrasound of the Thylacine embryos made the front-page, pushing sea-level statistics and the heat wave death tolls further back.

It turns out that creating an artificial womb is easier than implanting Thylacine eggs into living animals. Apparently this gives the scientists 'greater control over the crucial gestation period' and has nothing at all to do with the fact that the Numbat, the Thylacine's closest relative, hasn't been seen since late last year.

Watching the livestream, I had difficulty discerning the size of the womb. I know when Kangaroos are born, they're no larger than a jellybean. I imagine Thylacines aren't much different. The camera was fixed close on the womb and they set up a bright light on the other side so we could see through the translucent, plastic skin. Thylacines were not pack animals. They hunted in small family groups and did not produce large litters. Regardless, the artificial womb had thirteen distinct blobs floating in it.

Despite my reservations, I couldn't help but feel excited when it came time for the Thylacines to be born.

This quickly faded.

Shortly after their birth, each newborn Thylacine died. Their hearts were beating, they were healthy and alive, but they remained motionless and silent. They simply didn't breathe and so each one suffocated, one after the other, while I watched from behind my phone screen, completely helpless. It was like they had brought back the Thylacine so they could kill it all over again, drive it to extinction one more time just for good measure.

But the thirteenth Thylacine survived. I'm still watching it now, as its latched onto an artificial teat inside an artificial pouch, drinking what I have to assume is artificial milk.

When it was born, it didn't breathe either. The scientists quickly pried its mouth open and used a syringe to push air into its lungs. After that, it breathed on its own just fine. Almost one hundred and thirty years since its demise, the Thylacine is back.

I've spent my whole life waiting for this moment, and now that it's here I don't know what to feel.

*

The cloned Thylacine is almost fully grown now.

The media has dubbed it 'Benny', after the last natural Thylacine that died in captivity in 1936. Never mind the fact that the last Thylacine was actually female. Never mind that there is no evidence she was ever even called 'Benjamin'.

I still remember the first time I watched footage of her. It's old, of course — black and white, very grainy — and she is in a small concrete enclosure, the same one she would later die in.

Seeing that footage, I don't know how it was possible anybody ever saw a Thylacine and thought they looked anything at all like a tiger or a wolf. The only animal the Thylacine reminds me of is a Kangaroo. There is just something about the way they move their bodies that is so similar.

Of course, footage of 'Benny' can be found in abundance. High resolution videos of it are available all over the internet. I can't stand to watch them anymore.

The artificial Thylacine is perfectly healthy but, without human assistance, it would very quickly die. It still breathes on its own, ever since the initial assistance at its birth, but it does nothing else. It stands until it is physically manipulated into laying down. It lays down until it is lifted from the floor. It receives its sustenance intravenously because it does not chew. It's an animal without any instincts, a husk. It doesn't even blink. The scientists have to regularly apply saline to its lifeless eyes or they'll dry out.

Watching any footage of this so-called Thylacine makes my stomach turn.

Fittingly, this utterly apathetic creature has become the poster boy of Denialism. The people hellbent on downplaying the current environmental collapse point to the Thylacine as evidence that it won't be permanent.

If we have the power to bring things back later, why fight so hard to keep them alive now?

*

I've been having trouble sleeping lately.

I know many of us have. If it isn't the unrelenting heat, it's the mental toll we endure. The never-ending deaths, the bleak forecasts. My generation grew up with climate catastrophe on the horizon, we knew this was coming, but living through it is even worse than any of us imagined. I wish I knew how to quiet my mind.

My wife still manages to sleep through the night. She's always been a heavy sleeper. Her snores have been a comfort to me for forty years now. I know I couldn't do this without her, couldn't survive.

*

Sometimes when I wake in the night, I can't move my body.

I've heard about sleep paralysis before, of course, but had never experienced it until recently. It's an ordeal. I'm forced to lie there, completely conscious, but unable to do anything other than stare at the ceiling.

It reminds me of the artificial Thylacine.

Often, when I do get back to sleep, I have nightmares about that. I picture I'm trapped in its body. Conscious, but unable to move. The scientists' hands are on me, guiding my four legs, making me run. One of them grips my jaws and pulls them into a gaping yawn.

*

There is something in the room.

I can't see it, can't turn my head, but I know it's there. I can feel it.

I have more or less become accustomed to my sleep paralysis. I've learnt ways to cope with it and my nightmares have diminished, but this is new, this unshakable impression that I'm being watched, that there's a presence in the room.

When I regain control of my body, I turn my head so fast that my neck hurts. I scan the bedroom, but there's nothing there. It's empty.

I turn on my side and stretch my leg backwards until the heel of my foot touches my wife's bare calf. This is the extent of the contact we can tolerate during these hot winter nights, but it is a great comfort to me nonetheless.

*

My sleep paralysis is less frequent now.

It's no longer every night, but when it does happen, I always sense a presence. Right now, I can see it in the corner of my eye. There's a light coming from the doorway, bright but gentle like the moon's. I'm not scared like I usually am, only curious.

When the paralysis fades, I turn my head slowly and for a moment I think I see a Thylacine, sitting by the bedroom door. I blink and it's gone.

It remains imprinted on my eyelids for a few seconds more, like the afterimage from staring at a bright light.

*

When I awake tonight, the Thylacine is there.

Not in the doorway, but beside the bed. It's staring at me. I can't stare back, can't move. After an hour, it moves. It climbs onto the bed, laying across my body horizontally. Instantly I know it's her, the last Thylacine. She's made of a bluish white light that I can see through if I try. She lowers her head and falls asleep and, moments later, I do too.

*

Like all of their deaths, the last Thylacine's could have been avoided.

She was kept in Hobart Zoo, a spectacle for uninterested guests. She was locked out of her den during the day, forced to stand on the hard concrete where she could be seen. The Zoo staff sometimes forgot to unlock the den at night, and so she had to suffer the cold.

This is ultimately how she died. Exposed to harsh weather, crying out and desperate for warmth.

*

She visits me every night now and lays across my body.

I've heard of sleep paralysis demons before. I know some sufferers of sleep paralysis feel a weight on their chests and hallucinate something there, the cause of their inability to move. But I can't think of her as a demon, or even as a hallucination.

When the Thylacine lays on me, I feel no weight, as if she is only made of air, but I do feel the temperature of her body.

She's so cold.

With her keeping me cool during these unbearably warm nights, I'm able to sleep more peacefully than I have in months. It comforts me to know that as she cools me, I warm her. Finally, after all these years, the last Thylacine has found the warmth she's been so desperately looking for.

*

Some nights, I fight back sleep just so I can look at her longer.

She is the most beautiful sight I have ever seen, and to be able to admire a Thylacine up close — a real one — is a privilege that I alone am rewarded. I want so badly to reach out and pet her, but her presence is always accompanied by sleep paralysis. When I wake in the morning, she's gone. My wife has yet to catch so much as a glimpse of her.

Tonight, while I am admiring the Thylacine, I feel the paralysis gradually fade and movement return to my body. Slowly, inching my hand forwards bit by bit, I touch her. My fingertips move straight through her body. All I feel is the cold.

She must feel something, however, because she moves, turning her head to look at me. We stare into each other's eyes for a moment before she stands up and, hopping off the bed, leaves the room.

I do not hesitate to follow, not even stopping to put on shoes. She walks through the walls of the house and out the front door with ease. I open it and step out onto the street in nothing but my nightie. She doesn't run, but she isn't slow either. I have trouble following her down the streets, especially in the heat.

I'm forced to stop, to lean against a fence, and catch my breath.

The Thylacine keeps walking and I feel a deep anguish. I don't know why, but I think that this could be the last time I ever see her. If I lose her now, she'll never return.

I try to push on but I only make it a few steps before I have to stop again. I'm sweating. My knees ache, an unwelcome reminder that I'm no longer young.

She keeps walking and I watch her go. She's brighter than the streetlights she passes under. When she reaches the end of the street, she stops. She sits and watches me patiently, a beacon in the dark.

I know she's waiting for me.

She has something she wants me to see.

Slowly, I follow her. Whenever I'm forced to stop, she waits for me at the end of whatever street we're on. I don't have to think hard to realise where she's leading me. The scrub. The only part of this town that's the way it used to be. No houses or roads or shops, the scrub is a pocket of native wildlife, trees, and bushes. An Old Place.

When we're almost there, I can see bright light ahead. The trees are lit from below, their branches and leaves standing out in stark contrast to the night sky. It's like the moon has melted, dripping thick globules of its light down to the earth where they've pooled at the base of these trees.

When I finally reach the scrub, I'm rewarded with the stunning sight of a sea of light, waves of it constantly crashing in all directions. The Thylacine is sitting beside me. My eyes struggle to adjust to what I'm seeing. I can't discern the shifting shapes. A moment later the last Thylacine walks into the light and I finally realise what it is.

Thylacines.

Thousands of them, all made from the same bright light as the one that led me here. Some are walking, some are sitting or lying down, others are running and playing. All of them are passing through one another, passing through the trees and the bushes as if they aren't really there. The sight is overwhelming. It moves me to tears.

I wade out into this pool of Thylacines and my legs are instantly engulfed in the coolness of their bodies, of their kind light. I sit with my back against a paperbark tree and enjoy the refreshing sensation. It's a relief. They pass through me without hesitation. Eventually, one approaches me and gently lays across my legs. I know it's her.

Staring at her, I think of 'Benny', the artificial Thylacine that's out there right now in some lab in Sydney, and I finally realise what it is, why it has no instincts, no autonomy. Why it isn't even really alive.

'Benny' is a body, nothing more.

That's all the scientists have created. They couldn't revive the Thylacine, not truly. A body needs a soul, a spirit.

I realise that that's what I am surrounded by now. Thousands of spirits, the remaining remnants of the last true Thylacines.

I make a vow to the Thylacine laying on my lap. I whisper to her, to all of them, a promise. I tell them that I will never give them up. I will never tell anybody where to find them. I will never give the whitefellas a chance to study them, a chance to learn how to catch the spirit of a Thylacine and bind it to the body, to imprison it in their soulless creation.

The Thylacine are gone, extinct, and they have more than earnt their rest.

Dispatch

ZENA CUMPSTON

The Moreton-Robinson Annual Address
Barak University BLAKFULLAS Campus

Delivered by
Professor Zena Cumpston
(National Sky Ranger Program)
9 July 2029

As we celebrate the first five years of the Barak University
BLAKFULLAS Campus (Blak Lives And Knowledge
Fundamentals University for Living knowledge Living
culture And Solidarity), it is useful to reflect on our journey
so far and to mark a path for our future. The events which
led to the formation of this world-renowned Aboriginal
Institution were difficult and remain contentious. The huge
loss of lives, violence and upheaval of the first part of this
decade were traumatic for all. It is, however, important to

acknowledge that these difficult times have also forged a path towards many gains, not the least of which has been the establishment and ratification of meaningful Treaty in Victoria.

Following the significant loss of life due to COVID-19 across 2020, 2021 and 2022, the Aboriginal community found themselves in a rare, privileged position having largely survived the carnage. Over time, it became apparent that our ability to navigate and survive the COVID-19 crisis was a direct result of the efficacy of our grassroots community services, evolved from a sustained historical deficit in government services. Put simply: we've always had to fend for ourselves when it has come to empowering, protecting and advocating for our own communities, our own survival. Those who had, in the past, enjoyed almost unlimited protection and resourcing from the government were left completely vulnerable when governments repeatedly and catastrophically failed them. The wider Australian community did not have the means or networks to mobilise in the way Aboriginal community was able to.

For us, as Aboriginal people, everything revolves around and is underpinned by our communities, by systems of respect and communal decision making. These core beliefs greatly assisted our ability to mitigate harm. We quickly and effectively mobilised ourselves and worked as a community to meet challenges on every front. Conversely, the wider non-Aboriginal community experienced horrendous outcomes. These outcomes can be linked, in part, to the very problematic world view fundamental to the capitalist structure at the core of their human interactions. This world view entitles the individual over the whole and, too often, effects a climate of privilege which promotes a disregard for the greater good.

The mass deaths, the breakdown of government authority, and the erosion of the capitalist system are still having repercussions in Australia and across the world. But many new ways of being and doing have emerged as a direct result of this widespread chaos. The establishment of BLAKFULLAS Campus in Melbourne in 2024 can be seen to have risen from the flames of this devastating social and political landscape.

When universities either frantically closed, or spasmodically contracted, tens of thousands of jobs were lost almost overnight. Amongst the first to go were Aboriginal academics and staff members, the victims of predominantly insincere schemes to create parity. These schemes had barely gained traction despite decades of hard work by many both inside and outside the Aboriginal community. In the absence of government funding, those universities that reopened did so with the 'benevolent patronage' of mining companies, the same companies which had persistently shown a wilful disrespect for Aboriginal cultural sites. As the government pushed through laws to support the companies' ventures — which were now almost entirely underpinning all aspects of the Australian economy — the companies began to demonstrate a psychotic malevolence in their prolific desecrations and plundering. Aboriginal academics found themselves not only not being offered work in these now (again) openly elitist, morally bereft and racist institutions, the very few who were offered work could not accept it on moral, political and cultural grounds.

As with all successful Aboriginal services, the BLAKFULLUS Campus began with a small group of people who identified the need to empower our communities. Working together to specifically mobilise the vast network of incredible Aboriginal and Torres Strait Islander academics, researchers and support staff, now discarded by the tertiary system, in January of 2024 the first classes began in Collingwood in a disused former hotel. Aboriginal and Torres Strait Islander academics, not then yet on the universal wage that was implemented across Australia in 2025, volunteered to teach courses in areas identified as potential boom industries. For example, Cultural Land Management/Fire has, since inception, had a 100% success rate in employment. It is a booming industry largely as a result of the atomic bomb-like bushfires of 2020, 2021, 2022,

2023 and 2025. Biodiversity Management has also produced highly desirable and skilled First Nations graduates. These graduates have almost unlimited work opportunities due to the surge in rooftop gardens necessitated by urgent efforts to mitigate catastrophic urban thermal mass, and the continual failure of electricity grids across every major city. Our Urban Indigenous Rangers proved themselves far superior in their knowledge and capabilities in this field. They were highly adept in managing this new 'Country in the Sky' which saw more than 400 hectares of roof space in urban areas converted to green roof spaces between 2024 and 2028. The demand for our Urban Indigenous Rangers was also bolstered greatly by the inability of introduced crops and established agricultural systems to cope with dramatic climate fluctuations. Widespread food shortages highlighted the need to look to climate-stable indigenous plants and sustainable Aboriginal cultural food practices. Rooftops across the city now grow indigenous grain crops. The courses provided at BLAKFULLAS produced far superior graduates due largely to the on-Country learning from Elders fundamental to the structure of all BLAKFULLAS courses.

By the start of 2025, BLAKFULLAS had more students than could now be accommodated. With the introduction of the universal wage that year, it became possible for BLAKFULLAS to employ many more academics and therefore offer more courses. The campus needed to expand.

Driven by the wishes of the wider Australian society to harness the opportunities which come with rebuilding a society, the government was forced to enact the National Truth Telling Commission. The scope of the Commission also extended to reparations for stolen wages. Companies, including many whose massive wealth came from the pastoral industry, were called to account for their participation in slavery. Forensic accountants worked with historians and others to meticulously pore over financial records dating back more than 180 years. Landholdings were sold to meet reparation orders, and it was through one such sale in Victoria that the Wurundjeri mob received a significant payout. The Wurundjeri community, acknowledging the work of BLAKFULLAS in providing employment and training for a huge number of Aboriginal community members (which was, and is, resulting in dramatically better health and equity outcomes), gifted $80 million of their reparation monies to BLAKFULLAS. This money was used to buy a tract of land along the Merri Creek at Coburg. Starting in a shed as the new campus was built, classes continued and many more faculties were added.

As the demand for indigenous grain crops grew, the need to use old knowledge and develop new systems of processing for large populations became apparent. The Unaipon School of Engineering opened as part of BLAKFULLAS at the end of 2026. It quickly gained international attention due to its many successful programs aimed at empowering and illuminating Aboriginal innovation and sustainable practice. The School's reputation was further enhanced when the now famous Pascoe Kangaroo Grass Mill was designed and patented by the inaugural class of 2026. It was adopted as the machine-of-choice for the production of the now-highly popular kangaroo grass bread, soon to be exported across the world.

Central to the new campus was an extensive Aboriginal garden which provided on-Country learning for many of the emerging faculties. Perhaps the most impressive of these is the Healing Centre devoted to training a new generation of doctors, nurses and health-care professionals. This cohort bring new hope in efforts to Close the Gap, especially given there are more than 1500 Aboriginal and Torres Strait Islander students currently enrolled in more than 15 specialist courses in this faculty devoted to the health and wellbeing of Aboriginal and Torres Strait Islander peoples. The garden has also proved a valuable resource for the on-Country learning across all emerging faculties including the Agriculture Faculty, opened in 2027, and the Law Faculty, also opened in 2027. The Law Faculty has a particular focus on the Intellectual Property rights of communities in relation to the pharmaceutical and food industries.

As well as the industries which have boomed and been serendipitous to the strengths, interest and skills of Aboriginal communities, another huge aspect of the success and continual growth of the Barak University BLAKFULLAS has been the strength of the mandate on which it was founded. The mandate could be described as nuanced, extensive and reflexive. It can be best understood through its first two foundational principles: 'When we look after Country, Country looks after us' and 'Do no harm'. The principle of looking after Country reflects our essential role as custodians. The principle of 'Do no harm' speaks specifically to the colonial history of knowledge production in the Australian context. Research has outlined the extensive damage done to Aboriginal peoples through not only exclusion but also in the establishment of many harmful ideological beliefs such as Dying Race Theory, borne from the 'work' of academics that has dominated government policy since Invasion.

The mandate of the Barak University BLAKFULLAS also, importantly, cements structural systems which reflect Aboriginal and Torres Strait Islander ways of knowing, doing and being. All decisions are made as a community, with our community Elders providing guidance and support. Our teaching and research practice is embedded in positionality and works to decolonise knowledge production through empowering and resourcing our systems of knowledge. Whilst all of our academic, research and support staff and students are currently Aboriginal and Torres Strait Islander peoples, it is hoped that in the future we may offer some courses and opportunities for our allies from the wider Australian community, most especially as part of the recommendations made from the (National) Langton Truth Telling Report of 2026.

Ten years ago, it would have been difficult to believe the journey of this institution and the empowerment it has enabled for Aboriginal and Torres Strait Islander community. We still have many challenges, including many ongoing disagreements between community members, but more horizontal systems of governance in line with our traditional systems mean these problems are often easier to manage than they have historically been when we have been forced to work in western hierarchical systems. With our financial position underpinned by the outright ownership of our extensive campus all courses are currently free and it is hoped this will remain the case, especially as the universal wage has been guaranteed until 2070. There are plans afoot to open more faculties and provide specialist training in several more areas. The gains in health and wellbeing through the improved employment opportunities of our targeted areas of learning as well as the graduates which are soon to enter mainstream systems, especially those related to health and environmental management, are a huge source of pride and achievement for all associated with BLAKFULLAS.

We are greatly saddened by the many events which necessitated our inception but grateful that we have found a new platform to strengthen and empower our communities. In light of the incredible growth and productivity of BLAKFULLAS over the last five years, we look forward to the journey of the next five years and the continued movement towards a safer and more equitable world in which to be an Aboriginal and Torres Strait Islander person.

This piece was originally created as a 'Dispatch from the Future', as part of Assembly for the Future for BLEED Festival in 2020, presented by Arts House, City of Melbourne and Campbelltown Arts Centre. Assembly for the Future is a project of The Things We Did Next, co-created by Alex Kelly & David Pledger and produced by Not Yet It's Difficult & Something Somewhere Inc. To delve into other Dispatches from the Future see https://www.thethingswedidnext.org/dispatches-from-the-future/

August 2029

GENEVIEVE GRIEVES

Welcome to the very first edition of the
Murrnong Community Dispatch.

The Governance Committee thought it would be a good idea to communicate news, ideas and opportunities in this rapidly changing world we share. We are welcoming many new members to our community, and hope this helps to ground new residents in our culture and practices.

We have also established this newsletter as we acknowledge a strong sentiment in our community, a feeling that we haven't taken enough time to celebrate the big changes and achievements we have made together, as a collective of some eleven thousand people across this region.

We have faced much adversity — the new forms of fire that started in the Fire Season of 2019–2020 that continue to ravage us, COVID-19 in all the waves we have experienced, and the steady degradation of our waterways and landscape through mismanagement and ignorance. It took adversity to bring us together, but we are grateful that these catalysts have brought with them positive change.

The Healing Ceremonies that began in 2022 were a big shift for us, starting the truth-telling and recognition of our shared past that we all so needed to begin the healing for people and Country. These ceremonies were a central element of our community's growth and they are a regular and constant part of our calendar. To find local healing ceremonies please visit the Portal.

Another big shift for us was the Green Change of 2023 — where we welcomed many new community members from the cities. As we all know, this has helped our region thrive, not just with the numbers of people now calling this place home, but also all the many cultures that have come to be part of our community. The closing of refugee detention centres in late 2023 also brought a lot of new residents and we've become home for many more political and climate refugees since then — bringing new life and energy to what was once considered a dying region. Please visit the Portal to hear stories of our community or to share your story.

2024 saw the first meeting of our local Governance Committee. This first Committee was formed from Mutual

Aid groups established to respond to the many crises we faced and included many women, carers and people from diverse cultural backgrounds. We all found this shift to local decision-making had a big positive impact on our lives. It was also very welcome to have new voices involved in decision-making — such a variety of ages, skill-sets, cultural backgrounds, all coming together at a grassroots level to develop a future for our region. The First Peoples Elders Council was crucial in framing the agenda for this committee — shifting the region from thinking short-term to planning for generations in the future. Nominations for the 2030 Governance Committee are now open — please make your nomination in the Portal.

The Universal Wage brought in during the eleventh COVID wave in 2025 furthered the foundations for our new community structure — allowing us to allocate people to the jobs that needed doing such as Elder and Youth Care, Community Arts and Land Healing. Of course, none of this would have been possible without the relationships that have evolved between First Peoples Custodians and the rest of the community. One of our proudest achievements is the establishment of the First Peoples Land Handback scheme by our Governance Committee in that same year.

These changes have all been happening here on the ground and we have managed to survive and thrive, but we have had some difficulty aligning our new system with the federal government's representation of us. However, the new coalition government elected in 2026, under the stewardship of Penny Wong, has openly supported our new structure (and the structure of other regions who share this model) and we eagerly await the time when we can send our representative to Canberra to help us make the changes we want for our region and nation.

In the meantime, we continue the work of living respectfully on Country and through this, supporting our own survival. Last month was a very busy time — we've moved into the fifth season of our local calendar which sees the return of the kingfishers to their nests, the laying of turtle eggs and the seventh burn in our cycle, focussing on maintenance of kangaroo grass and murrnong along the creeks and waterways.

It was amazing — once again — to see small plumes of smoke everywhere as the controlled burns rolled out across our region. We all know that this means increased safety for us as we come into our next Fire Season and that Country is being cared for the way it should be. Congratulations to all the Fire groups for another successful month of coordinated burns and a very special thanks to the First Peoples Elders Council for sharing this knowledge with all of us. Express your personal thanks in the Portal or in person at your local community dinner this week.

The Land Healing groups are making incredible progress

doing the work needed to care for Country as we have been taught and guided by our Senior Custodians. Each group's Elders are busy making plans for the next season's work with their apprentices managing the workload of creating teaching materials and administering their activities. They are moving as fast as they can, trying to mitigate the many challenges on the horizon as we have already faced some heavy losses with patches of Country beyond repair. We are all very grateful for their continuing hard work which is so central to our survival on this Country. If you would like to change your job allocation and move to a Land Healing group we have two new groups starting soon on land east of the river. Register your interest in the Portal.

Take care everyone and look after one another. Fire Season starts soon and more severe weather warnings are on the horizon — we all need to be extra vigilant and have our local event plans ready to be activated when needed. Keep connected with your local network and stay safe.

Genevieve Grieves
Steward, Murrnong Community

This future was generated by Genevieve, Joseph, Carissa and Tara in a collective workshop as part of a 'Dispatch from the Future', as part of Assembly for the Future for BLEED Festival in 2020, presented by Arts

House, City of Melbourne and Campbelltown Arts Centre. Assembly for the Future is a project of The Things We Did Next, co-created by Alex Kelly & David Pledger and produced by Not Yet It's Difficult & Something Somewhere Inc. To delve into other Dispatches from the Future see https://www.thethingswedidnext.org/dispatches-from-the-future/

The Debt

CHEMUTAI GLASHEEN

Imani jogged through the bush park on her way home from school. She ducked to avoid the large branches which drooped over the beaten track. A gecko was sunning itself on a recently fallen tree.

'Whoa!' She crouched and scooped it up, allowing herself to be drawn into the eyes that stared back at her. 'Couldn't be bothered to hide, huh?'

Imani stroked the white strip along its back all the way to the fat tail. She loved getting into a staring contest with geckos. They made her feel like a hero in their show.

'How adorable you are! For now, you are Mr Gecko until we get to know each other a little more, right?'

He chirped at her. She let him run up her arm and on to her shoulder before he disappeared inside her blouse.

'That tickles! Ooo …'

Behind her, a bell rang. Imani sprung around, lost her footing and fell back, landing on her backside on the stony path. She squeezed her eyes shut, waiting for the pain to abate. She felt Mr Gecko crawl on her chest. Her eyes flew open to find him making his way onto her forearm. She beamed at him as she struggled into a sitting position.

'You okay, Mr Gecko?' She cooed at him.

Imani turned around to say something to the bicycle rider, but there was no one in sight. She rose, a little unsteady at first, and made her way home. She was rummaging through her bag to find her house keys when she noticed that the door was slightly ajar. She hesitated. At this end of town, doors were always bolted tight. She nudged the door open, kicked her shoes off and called out to Mum.

She was halfway into the front room before she was jolted to a stop. Something felt different. Her wandering gaze swept the room. The cold of the floor tiles permeated through her school tights. Floor tiles? Radiant white tiles, which looked like they had a generous sprinkling of coconut flakes, filled the floor space. The dirt-coloured carpet, worn out by drunken dancing, was gone.

'Wow, Mum!' she called out. 'Finally!'

Mother always wanted to redecorate the house. Something always stopped her — but never money. Mother often bragged that finding money was her hidden talent. Imani was marvelling at the changes when she heard Mother come into the room.

'Wha—' the words died in her throat.

Mother was in a wheelchair.

'Amani, good you are here. How about pilau for dinner?

Pick some green cardamom from the garden.'

Mother turned and wheeled herself back into her bedroom. Imani raced after her.

'Are you now training on wheelchairs?'

'Amani, what is with the silly questions?'

Mother scowled at her, but Imani's attention was on the brightly coloured headscarves hanging on a set of hooks just inside the door. That was new. She recognised the black and red rooster logo of the Sauti Sol band. A tiny smile sneaked up on her. Without thinking, she picked up the scarf and tied it loosely around her neck. She turned to her left to find a mirror but the dresser had been moved. That is when she really saw the room. The bed was in the middle of the room. Above it was something that looked like a lift attached to a form of railing which went around the bed frame. The room seemed bigger — no, the bed seemed smaller. The clothes and shoes that resided on the floor — gone. Spilling over a white dresser was a plant, probably an ivy.

'A couple of bottles of hand sanitisers on the wall,' Imani chuckled, 'and Mum, this could be a hospital room!'

'Amani,' Mother snapped, 'the cardamom ain't going to pick itself, ala!'

Mother was beginning to swear, so Imani fled the room. All that cleaning must have gone to her head if she expected Imani to make anything more complex than a boiled egg. What was cardamom anyway? Imani went past the kitchen and sat on the back doorsteps. She looked out to the newly trimmed shrubs which backed onto the community gardens. The grass between the rectangular herb gardens had been cut. It was the first time since Father moved out that the garden had received any attention. Something crawling around her waist reminded her that she was not alone. She reached around the folds of her school skirt and drew Mr Gecko out. She stroked his belly for a while before she became aware that he did not seem at ease like all her other geckos.

'What Mr G, did my mother startle you as well?'

He blinked back at her.

'Haiya!' She jumped back, trying to shake the gecko off but he clung on. He blinked at her again. She took a deep breath and drew him in for a closer examination.

'Eyelids! You aren't supposed to have eyelids!' She squinted at the gecko. She turned him over and examined his feet. They were clawed.

'You are not a gecko!'

An uneasiness rose in her and her body shook. What is wrong with me? She knew she had picked up a gecko. Geckos were family to her. She would never mistake a lizard for a gecko. But something was amiss. It took a moment for her brain to catch up. The trimmed shrubs. The tiles. Mother's bedroom. Her skin began to tingle, her mouth went dry. Mother called her Amani!

'No. No. No.'

Imani rose slowly, her head shaking of its own volition.

Her feet propelled her to Mother's room. She stood at the doorway, partially hidden, and watched. Mother was poring over some paperwork. Without looking up, Mother reached back into her wheelchair bag and drew out a folder. She made a strangled sound as her right hand flew to clutch her left shoulder. With gritted teeth, she grabbed a pen to scribble some notes. Her right hand never left her left shoulder. Imani rubbed her eyes. Either her eyes were deceiving her or she was looking at her mother's reflection! Mother was writing with her left hand: the painful one! Imani steadied herself against the bedroom door.

'Mum?' Her voice barely above a whisper.

She took a few tentative steps towards her mother. Her eyes on Mother's plain black headscarf. A few grey hairs poked from underneath the scarf and fell over the old fern-like scar. Oh God! Mother didn't have that scar. Bile rose in her throat. But this was Mother! Her mother! Same look. Same face. Same voice.

'Amani!' Mother snapped.

'It's Imani.' She wiped her clammy hands on her skirt.

'What's that, dear?' Her mother asked, her eyes finding Imani's. They squinted and then widened.

Mother and daughter seemed to freeze. Expressions crossed from one face to another. Mouths opened. Words failed.

'You … you are not my daughter!' Mother swallowed audibly.

Imani sank, expelling air as her butt hit the floor. Mother's hands gripped the chair. Both women held the other's gaze hostage.

'Who are you?' The one who looked like Mother broke the silence first.

'And who are you?'

'What have you done to my daughter?'

'Wh—, no, I didn't … I don't know what is happening.'

Imani's vision blurred. Her eyelids heavy, she eased into the blackness.

When she opened them, a bottle of water was in her hand. This time, when she found the eyes of the woman who bore her mother's face, there was something else in them: a gentleness her own mother did not have.

'Where … er … what is this place?'

Lookalike Mum motioned to her to drink some water.

'You are in Reap Town.'

You mean Sow Town. The words didn't leave Imani's lips. She got to her feet, patting her pockets for her phone. The GPS would know where she was. Dang! No signal. She tapped it a few times, holding it high above her head, as she walked around the room. Still — nothing! Lookalike Mum unlocked her own phone and then passed it to Imani. Reap Town came up immediately but there was nothing about Sow Town. She zoomed out and the surrounding towns of Kericho and Kisumu came into focus. They were where they were meant to be. The River Nile, meandering away from

Lake Victoria, also came into view. The country, and the entire east African region was the same, but Sow Town was missing. In its place was the Town of Reap.

'This is wrong. The map is wrong!' Hysteria crept into her voice. She chugged down the rest of the water.

'Sip it slowly.' Lookalike Mum held out another bottle for her. 'What's with the lizard that keeps popping in and out of your clothes?'

Imani managed a small smile. 'That's Mr Gecko.'

'So, your mum has my face.' It was stated rather than asked.

Imani nodded, her attention on the wheelchair. 'This is real?'

'I haven't been in it very long,' she said, giving the wheel a quick tap. 'Since New Year.'

'Ah, six months.'

'No, about eleven.'

'The New Year of this year? But we are only halfway into the year.'

Imani looked at Lookalike Mum's phone again. The date read Mon, 4 Pagume.

'Pagume! What is that?'

'You don't have much of an education, do you? You can't add and you don't know your months of the year.'

Lookalike Mum's chuckle irritated her. Imani sank onto the floor with a sigh. She felt around the hand rim of the wheelchair.

'Makes you uncomfortable, doesn't it?' Lookalike Mum asked.

Unsure how to respond, Imani held her tongue. Silence fell between them. It stretched on like a rubber band; the sting of the snap back threatened.

'It's New Year's Day.' Lookalike Mum sounded expressionless. 'I am getting ready to go out with friends. I hear a crack in my bones. Pain across my lower back. Sudden, like a branding by a hot iron. There is pain everywhere. I collapse. My legs cannot move. Have never walked since.'

Imani's eyes widened. Not only did she disbelieve the story, but no way could such a story be told so simply. When Mother told a horror story, you bled at the mention of blood.

'See this deep cut?' Lookalike Mum rolled up her sleeve. 'Same incident.'

The calmness of her voice was belied by the veins in her neck which seemed ready to pop.

'You are s-s-scaring me!' Imani hid her face in her hands.

'I'm scared too. But I need to know. So many mysterious bruises keep happening to me.'

Lookalike Mum shifted slightly in the chair. She leaned in and lifted Imani's face with her index finger. Had Imani stumbled into the centre of a maze with invisible walls? She fixed her eyes on the scar on Lookalike Mum's arm. Tentatively, she reached across and touched the scar. Her hand sprung back.

'You are cold.' She attempted an explanation. 'My mother is never cold.'

'Uhm.' Lookalike Mum's eyes narrowed briefly, as she felt Imani's arm. Then after a small hesitation, 'What does your mother do?'

'She is … um … with the motorbike police.'

Lookalike Mum dropped Imani's arm like it was a burning ember. Something altered in her. The gentleness from earlier — gone. On Imani's belly, Mr Gecko tensed; everything stilled — beating heart, rushing blood and the noises in her head.

'The doctors said my spinal injury was consistent with being hit by a motorcycle. The heavy kind used by the police.'

Imani hugged her knees tight. Surely her mother's job had nothing to do with Lookalike Mum's accident? She opened her mouth to say something but instead, the horrifying headlines came flooding back. New Year — news on TV — university riots — police drag woman out of car — woman's spine broken. But the dates did not match up.

'The dates do not match up,' Imani said, more to herself than to Lookalike Mum.

The news had not named any of the police officers involved in the New Year's incident. Mother never spoke about her work. But she remembered the outrage from the crowd, on the news. Stop Killer Police! Dirty Cops on Bikes! Flawed Law!

Gripped by trepidation, Imani found her feet. She had to move. She took a few steps back and bumped into the door. The door swung shut. She spun around. She went hot. She went cold. Smiling back at her, was herself. On the back of the door, hung her family portrait — an equivalent same face family. Her brain emptied of all thoughts. Somehow, her body remembered to breathe.

'My husband is no longer with us,' Lookalike Mum's voice came from afar.

If Lookalike Mum said anymore, Imani did not hear it. Compelled, her hand reached for the portrait. Her fingers stayed on the same face as hers. Her thoughts held at bay before, broke — threatening to blow her mind. Do we look alike or are we the same person?

'Somehow this is your mother's doing. My bruises, scars and broken bones. Your being here gives me the answers I have been waiting for.'

Despite the shrieking in her head, Imani could not disbelieve that her mother had inflicted pain on someone. It is what Mother did. But Lookalike Mum's woes — that did not make sense. Even Mother at her coldest, would not touch a reflection of herself.

'But how?'

'What you do in your world has real consequences in ours.'

Imani flinched. How does one respond to such an accusation when she was not sure if she was still standing in the same skin or under the same sky?

'You recognised the scar on my arm, didn't you?'

Imani nodded.

'I want to hear you say it.'

'It … er … sh-she … Mother did not mean to. She was doing her job. She pulled a suspect out of a car.'

'Uh-uh!' Lookalike Mum spat out. 'She dragged an innocent woman through broken glass! You want to know how I know she was innocent?'

Imani braced herself. When Mother was angry, she was a bulldog. Her eyes flared and her words stung as much as the crack of her hand across your face. Imani sat on her hands to stop them from trembling.

'My body pays the price.' The voice that squeezed out of Lookalike Mum's clenched jaw was calm. 'Sorry to do this to you child, but there is a reason you need to know. This is a warning.'

Imani was already exhausted by shock and bewilderment. If this was a dream, she needed to wake up, pronto. Her eyes watered.

'Every time your mother commits an act of injustice, it counts as a debt which my world pays. But now, the term of the loan is up. When you leave, the door to our world will forever be closed to you and your family.'

'Huh?'

'That means, if there is one more innocent life taken, the consequences will ricochet off the victim and onto your own family. My family is no longer whole. We cannot absorb anymore punishment.'

Something went off inside of Imani's abdomen, sending her blood rushing in every direction. Her heart was pounding. The ground turned to miry clay. The thoughts in her head picked up speed. Mr Gecko appeared on her arm. He raised his head and barked. She needed air. She stumbled out. Out of the room, out of the house.

Once outside, she started running. My father, my poor father! She was in full sprint when she realised she did not know where she was going. Where was home? How did she get here? She slowed to a stop. Oh, I am done for! She needed a moment. She sank to a squat on the side of the road and dropped her head into her hands.

'Think Imani, think. How did you get here?'

Mr Gecko slithered down her side and scurried across the road. Imani chased after him. Just then, a bicycle bell rang out to warn her — but it was too late. Imani fell face down on the ground.

'Watch—' she turned angrily to the rider.

There was no rider. There was no bicycle in sight! Mr Gecko chirped. Imani reached for him.

'You okay?' He responded by sticking out his tongue to lick his eye.

'Whoa! Your eyelids are gone. What …?'

She jumped onto her feet as her eyes swept all around her. It looked familiar. It felt familiar. The recently fallen tree across the path was still oozing sap. Mr Gecko was a gecko again. She blew out her cheeks to rouse herself from the nightmare. She headed home, her step lighter.

'Ping!' Her phone notification came on.

She had a signal! A signal! She whipped out her phone to check her GPS location. Town of Sow, it said. Phew, she was home. She moved the gecko onto her left wrist and watched him crawl up her arm. Their stares locked in affection before Mr Gecko crawled up her shoulders and then disappeared under her scarf.

'My wh…at!'

She jolted to a stop. With trembling fingers, she ripped the scarf from her neck. Oh God! The whole nightmare was real. As real as the Sauti Sol scarf in her hand. The woman with Mother's likeness had said that the term of the loan was up. She had to stop Mother, or she would lose her father and herself. But how? What was she going to say to Mother? That a parallel world to theirs exists! That there was a Town of Reap and that they used a different calendar. She was barely able to explain the phenomenon to herself, how could she explain it to someone else? She lumbered home trying to contain her fear. She swallowed the rising panic. They were in debt and someone was coming to collect.

Song of the Nawardina

MAREE McCARTHY YOELU

Long ago
adv. wulabut-wulabut

Wulabut-wulabut, our special stories and songs, were sung with towering strength; echoing across the lands and seas, transported by the animals, the wind and the nawardina.

No matter if you were on Wadjigany country or on foreign lands, you could hear the song of your people.

In 2020, much has changed — the lands have been slowly divided, taken for cattle stations and holiday homes. We now even have other occupants making their home on our Wadjigany country, professing their traditional ownership — but my elders only know them as foreigners. The destruction and tyranny has squashed the songs, the stories and pride of what was once a powerful and happy tribe.

This year, we have also seen bushfires and COVID-19; my people fighting yet another foreign invader.

It is time to get back to country.

At kulgamorra, sunset, a fluorescent orangey-red hue danced on the horizon. I sat with my Bapa, on my first night back on country. How good it felt to be home.

'Bapa, what if there was a way we could go back in time and visit our ancestors?' I asked.

The fire crackled in silence, while I waited for him to respond.

The fire was mesmerising, even at dusk, though the night was clearly arriving; it was almost like it was calling me in; welcoming me to dive between the embers' glow and the sparks flickering into the air.

It was almost like it was happy to see me.

What would I find between the flickers? If I dived in, would I find my answer?

Bapa often took a long time to respond. A long pause, a long sip of his cuppa tea.

He believed you would always find the answers in the silence, when you give your spirit a while to mati nya-mu, to sit still.

Bapa used to always tell me, 'you don't know how to sit still, you're always hurrying,' so this felt like a challenge to me. The truth is, he was right. I didn't know how to mati nya-mu.

'You can't find anything with a busy spirit, a busy mind, son.

'You can learn a lot from being still and listening to your country. He is teaching every day, you just got to be willing to listen. But I often imagine visiting our ancestors too, son. One day, I will, but not yet.'

I could hear the sparks louder now. Like they were dancing in support of my Bapa's words, fuelling their glow in the night.

I wonder if our ancestors ever wondered what the future would hold for them? Did they know their people would struggle with loss of language, stories and songs? Did they ever cry for the future?

Out of the silence, Bapa says, 'Nawardina.'

Nawardina is a kapok mangrove plant. It is used for many different things, but the wood burns well. The dry branches can also be used to carry fire, as they smoulder slowly, allowing fire to be carried to a new campsite.

Our ancestors would use nawardina often. It is a special tree; and it also has its own song.

If you learn its song, our people say, it will carry you to the past, where you'll be transported back in time. Our ancestors all live on the island of the dead.

My Bapa points directly ahead, to an island which lies a little way in front of us. 'That's the island there, we call it Rak Morragara, "the place of yesterday". Our people go back there, after they pass away. Our ancestors are not far and they are within reach; if you can learn the song of the nawardina, you can visit them, in their world.'

I realised I had to mati nya-mu now and listen to country. I wanted to learn the song of the nawardina, so I could carry it to the island of the dead where my people live in spirit, waiting for us to come sit with them and learn from them. I needed to reignite the language of my people. To bring the stories of the past into the present — for my sons and daughters, their children and so forth.

My ancestors can help me. I can feel it.

The fire still flickered bright; starting to warm me from the dry season air. I lay watching the yiletj, the flame, still inviting me to dive, heart first, straight in the fire.

So, I did.

Bonetj
n. dream
Bonetj-nga-yebe — 'I dream'

The embers glowed fluorescent orange and gold specks sparkled as they twirled around me, moving me in a circular motion until I was at the foot of tall man. He had a white unkempt beard, but it suited him. He was motioning me to come with him.

'Kawa,' he said.

Come.

So, I followed him; I instinctively trusted him with my entirety. It wasn't hard to, he looked a little bit like my Bapa, just older. I took his hand; and we walked down a sandy bush track, towards the sunset.

At the end of the track there were people dancing; it

looked like they were having wangga, corroboree. I could see the dust swirling in the orange sunset, from mununuk and mirak, from the man and woman dance. I could feel it on my skin, the clinging dust fragments welcoming me to wangga.

I could hear the song.

Tap, tap, tap, the clapsticks sounded.

The rumbling of the didgeridoo. The sound, so low and drone-like, it vibrated deep inside me, pulling me towards the earth.

Then I heard the voices, in a low chant, singing in my Language — Batjamalh.

I recognised only a few words, so I muttered to the wind, 'bibere-bene nye-me', 'whisper in my ear'.

The words came instantly. While I settled in the earth, I could hear the wind speak to me; but I cannot say it in English I must only speak it in Batjamalh.

What I can tell you, it was about letting the wind take you, to find your way.

My people continued to dance up a storm, singing the words to life, singing the songs to life, right in front of my eyes.

The old man led me over to the group of men that were dancing. Their movements were fluid like a river. Their legs and arms moved in unison. I watched and slowly joined in their dance. When the feet hit the earth on the beat, it felt like it was done with so much intention and pride. I instantly felt goosebumps, all over my body. This was more than just 'a dance'. This was culture, stories, language. This was my identity.

It is all intertwined, you cannot have one without the other.

I start to wake. Where am I? I feel my Bapa shaking my arm, telling me to go to bed.

The fire was still awake, keeping me company. It took me to my dreams of country. Bapa did say to be still. Listen to country. The song is still in my head; I tap the beat with my finger, so I don't forget the special song of the nawardina.

Bangany
n. song
Bangany-ung nye-bindjang nya-mu — 'keep singing a song'

Bapa would always say, 'keep singing a song'. That's how we'd always share our stories. Wulabut-wulabut, we'd share our significant stories, ceremonies and songs through spoken word, not with a pen and paper. We would often share paintings, but some have been destroyed now too.

But if there is anything my ancestors are asking me to do, that would be to bangany-ung nye-bindjang nya-mu, to keep singing a song.

I feel, I must. I feel a responsibility, for my people, to keep that song going, just like that song of the nawardina, that will carry me into our past world, or what my Bapa calls the island of the dead. That nawardina will carry that flame and keep me safe while I travel into the past.

The sun was rising above the kapok trees that stand tall, embracing our home. The morning birds tweeting, so excitedly from the canopies. Why have I taken so long to come home?

Bapa hadn't forgotten our conversation around the campfire. In fact, the next day he told me we would go and collect some nawardina, so we could go and visit our old people from the past.

Rak Yinymek, it's a place not far, we call it the fish bowl.

A place full of tucker, a seafood feast in a bowl.

The nawardina is here too; but you have to go on low tide; so that's what Bapa and I did. We headed to Rak Yinymek when the tide was going out.

Bapa told me that not just anyone can pick nawardina; it chooses you.

'If you have the right heart, the right intentions, our people will lead you to it.'

Bapa would always share their stories of country; especially when we were on it.

My senses were alight; it was like someone flicked a switch and I dived in and tasted the ocean, exploring the colourful coral and reef fish whizzing past.

The wind was gentle and danced around me while I looked beyond the fish bowl.

There was something magical occurring, as I searched

for the elusive nawardina; the wewiny, the spiral shells, were glistening along the beach. The sand was glowing quite beautifully along the shore; every now and then the sun would glimmer intensely too, off the golden sands of Rak Yinymek beach, shining its rays towards a mangrove bush in front of me. Then Bapa pointed to the path the rays had made, through the mangrove jungle. I walked first, through the sandy, mangrove mud; feeling quite unsure as I stepped slowly towards the beaming light. The beams seemed to be getting stronger with every step I took.

The wind was strong too, 'kawa' it called. Come! I knew the nawardina was close. I felt it.

And the songs that I heard in my dreams were strong again. Tap, tap, tap, of the clapsticks, the low tones of the didgeridoo, vibrating through my body. I felt my body gravitate towards the earth again; like it was pulling me in for an embrace.

The beaches of Rak Yinymek came alive. I had never seen it glisten like this before. I was starting to learn that our places were more than just fishing spots; they were special in other ways. Every tree, every shell, every rock, every bit of marine life — connect us to our past, our people, tradition, songs and stories. Just like the nawardina.

As I reached the centre of the mangrove forest, the light shone directly on the nawardina, where it stood sturdy and staunch. I never knew what it looked like before, but there was no denying this was it. It captured my eye as it danced in the breeze. I took a long branch off and put it carefully in my bag. I had this inner sense, that my ancestors were happy; I certainly was.

I couldn't stop thinking about the next part of my journey — to visit the island of the dead; where all our people travel once they pass. I just needed to remember the song from my dreams, the one my people showed me.

The song of the nawardina would show me the way.

Yik & berrangarang, 'Old & new'

I had the dream again: they're excited to see me; to teach me the old ways, of language, stories, traditions and songs. I'm excited too, but a little bit nervous. My Bapa says when you sing the song of the nawardina, our ancestors will hear it and they'll start singing too. Once our songs are synced, they open up the channel to their old world; allowing me to time travel my way there. It's like a portal opens, but only for a short while. In their world, time does not exist anymore; they are not restricted by time, for time is only something humans have to contend with. Even for me, regardless that I will be visiting a timeless world, I will still be limited to the time I have with my people.

Bapa says, 'You must not forget to light the nawardina, it'll keep your flame alight and you won't get lost while you journey.'

That evening, towards sunset, Bapa and I began the song of the nawardina.

Tap, tap, tap, the clapsticks sound.

My Bapa begins to play the didgeridoo; the sound so low and moving; the sound pulls me towards the earth.

Then, on the beat, I begin to sing, focussing on the song of the nawardina. I sing in a low, monotone voice, chanting the words of the song from my dreams:

'Nawardina! Come help me, find my way to my people.'

*

As the night closed in, I felt like I was shifted into another space, just like in my dreams. My nawardina was lit brightly and provided the special light I needed to guide me into the past.

It didn't take long, when I was greeted by the tall man again. This time he introduced himself as my Kuga (my Bapa's Father). He gave me a hug, as I could hear wangga in the distance. He took me by the hand and we set off towards the music. We followed the dark, sandy track towards the sound of the clapsticks. Only a hundred metres or so.

As we entered, there was a huge fire, plenty of laughter and dancing. Everyone was speaking in our Batjamalh language; no one there spoke a word of English. Oh how I wished to speak Batjamalh fluently.

'You will,' Kuga said. I was surprised, as I hadn't said this out loud.

After meeting with family, the first thing they did was take me to the water hole where they take all their living visitors — they splashed water on my belly-button and over my head, then wiped the remains over my forehead. It was refreshing. I've never felt more alive; which was a strange thing to feel, on the 'island of the dead'. I was emotional, almost mournful, but incredibly happy at the same time. How can I feel all of this at once?

There was a huge feast of sea-side goodness waiting for me. Saltwater prawns, crab, crayfish, squid, mangrove worm, trepang, oysters, long-bums, periwinkles and an array of fish. They had made it all just for me. They caught them in their warrngatj, (fish-nets) and with their barrkkata ngak, two-pronged fish spears.

The nawardina was still alight and burning strongly, while I listened to the voices of my people.

While we danced,

sang,

shared stories,

laughed,

cried,

spoke words in Language.

I was immersed in the songs and their spirit of giving; they were generous in every way.

They also spoke of their sadness, for the destruction in

today's world. They're sad their language is gone with them, their knowledge and traditional ceremonies not practised as much as they used to be. They cry for their Wadjigany people.

In fact they mourned, wailed with me. They were sad, as if their humans were dead already. Real tears and heartbreak could have extinguished the flames of my nawardina. But they were determined not to let my flame burn out.

That's when they told me about the eternal flame, which would allow me to keep the connection with them, so we could continue to learn and strengthen our Wadjigany culture.

'When you take the flame from the island of the dead back home, the flame will continue to burn from season to season,' Kuga said.

'Just put your nawardina in our flames and your nawardina will never die. You'll be able to visit us, whenever you need.'

It was hard to say goodbye, after only meeting my old people for the first time. But I knew in my heart, I didn't belong here. I had a job to do; the old people were relying on me to keep them alive in the berrangarang, the new.

I spent my last few hours before dawn wide awake and listening to my old people.

We talked into the night air, to the trees, to the wind, to the animals. Then Kuga spoke directly to my heart — not a word was spoken, not a sound came out of his mouth, but I felt it; thanks to Bapa for teaching me how to mati nya-mu and hear the most important things.

Kuga led me back down the sandy bush track, lit by the flames from the nawardina.

On the walk back, he reminded me of the eternal flame and how I'd be able to visit if I ever needed.

'The nawardina is special

For one, it has its own song

Two, it carries your flames from your world to mine

And three, many rafts and canoes are made from it. It's a seafarers dream, to have song, light and transport, all from the nawardina.'

*

I knew in my heart, my work was only just beginning and I had no idea what that looked like.

'It's time, my boy, time to light the way for our people on earth.'

I nodded and then the clapsticks returned. My nawardina was lit forever … I could find my way home. I felt I shifted and just like that I was gone … finding myself on the beach, in front of Bapa's place. I wondered if he even knew I left?

I see him, walking along the beach towards me, spear in one hand, with some freshly caught snapper in the other.

'Breakfast, son?'

'Sure Bapa, and maybe a cuppa … I can't wait to tell you all about my visit back to our old people.

The Breakup

JASMIN McGAUGHEY

'I have to break up with you,' I say, and I make sure to look Artie in the eyes as the words reluctantly leave my mouth.

He blinks slowly and leans away from me. 'Zillah …'

'I'm sorry,' I say and even though my heart hurts and my stomach heaves with queasiness, I don't flinch.

Artie's expressions change in front of me. Miniscule dips of the brow, a tremble of his lips, tightening in the jaw. His confusion and hurt are all there on his face.

We're sitting on the oval, under the poinciana tree towards the end of the field where my bus stop is. We usually meet here every afternoon to talk through the day and help each other out with homework before heading home. My sister, Nik, calls us nerds. Why aren't you getting laid at his place? She always asks me.

My legs are crossed, and I've placed my laptop bag in my lap so Artie and any passers-by can't see up my skirt and to the bright orange and purple love heart undies I'm wearing. Although it's cooling down, little bits of the left-over summer sun peep through the poinciana's foliage to heat up my hair. I've got them tight curls that soak up love from the sun and retain the heat.

'Is it—' Artie starts and then stops. He's got long lashes that cast mini shadows on his face. He flutters them slowly when he's thinking hard. 'Is it because of what I told you. Showed you?'

I nod.

Freaking superpowers. My boyfriend is an Edward-Cullen-Peter-Parker-Superman. He's got powers.

Two weeks ago, Artie took me to his place, a giant house with a heap of land and its own creek that weaved through surrounding bush and forest. It's near the northern beaches and took us forty minutes to get to.

He stood me in the fields of his home, spread his hands and levitated off the ground with blue sparks in his hands.

I've read and seen Twilight. I've watched Spiderman and read a lot of the comics. I know they're the good guys, and I know Artie is too.

At first when he showed me that he was strong enough to lift his car over his head and could fly around the house (he offered to take me for a ride to which I, of course, politely and vehemently refused) I was ecstatic.

'I've only had these gifts for about a year,' Artie told me when he touched down in front of me after a display of freaky aerobatic manoeuvres.

'A year?' I said.

Artie nodded and approached me slowly, like I was a wounded animal or something. He wrapped his big hands around my arms and squeezed gently. 'It feels so good to tell someone. To tell you.'

He'd kissed me then, lightly on the lips and then deeply, putting one hand around my waist and tightening the other through my hair.

I'd felt tingles and excitement and freakin pride too. My boyfriend was powerful.

But then I'd gone home and realised that every single emotion I'd felt had been born from shock. And it took me two weeks to sort through it all so I could understand my mind. And it took me two seconds to remember the promise I made my mother before I started high school. Don't date dangerous or stupid people.

Artie's not stupid. But he may be dangerous.

'That's— that's racist,' Artie reckons, jumping up on his feet and snapping me back to the now.

'It's not cos you're white,' I reply, standing up real slow in the hopes that my calm movements will help.

'Not that,' Artie spits, flashing me the most exasperated look ever. 'It is because I'm different though. Because I have this.' His hands splay out by his sides and the blue electricity appears over his fingers. Dancing.

'Artie,' I say, moving to his side and motioning for him to drop the laser show. He doesn't want to be spotted. That was the last thing he told me before he dropped me home that first time. 'Don't tell anyone, Lah.'

The crux of my problem.

I can't lie to my family.

It is an impossibility. Not an action that would be hard for me to do. But something I could never fathom. My lips physically wouldn't be able to form the lie. When I got home from his place those few weeks ago, and stared into the faces of my mother, uncles, little brother and big sister, the tight something in me had snapped. When my Aka and Athe had come over for tea, the other something in me had snapped too.

They would want to know my boyfriend had superpowers and there was no way I could lie to them.

I don't tell Artie this though. He wouldn't understand. His parents are super rich and super busy. They fly around the country (in planes, not with powers) looking over their hotels, their restaurants and all the other things they own. Artie's left alone most of the time, which is how he got the powers in the first place.

'I won't tell you where it is,' Artie said, as we strolled to his car after his first display, because — I dunno, I guess he didn't trust me with powers — 'but there's this thing, this technology thing. It was humming and sparking, and I touched it.'

'You touched it?' My jaw practically dropped to the ground and for a moment I was speechless. What kind of stupid person went out and touched the scary looking electrical unidentified object? (Maybe he was kinda stupid).

But it was yet another thing that was different between us.

'Artie,' I say now. 'It's just too much to deal with. Okay?'

'For you to deal with?' Artie steps back and his voice rises hysterically. 'I'm the one with the ... powers,' he whispers the last word at the sight of my worried glance.

'You seem pretty okay with it.'

'Okay with it?' Artie's voice has reached new heights now. Surely every dog and every human with supersonic hearing is having their eardrums busted up.

'I'm sorry, Artie. I ... I've got things going on.'

'Then tell me about it. We're not the couple who just avoids tough conversations,' he says. He begins pacing and throwing me dark looks that say more than his words ever could. He is right. We've always been honest and open. We've talked about our hopes and dreams (and all the cliché bullshit), we've talked about sex and when we want to have it, about each time we've hurt and everything that makes us happy. He's met my family for God's sake and that's huge. I have close life-long friends who don't even know what the inside of my house looks like.

'Zillah.' Artie's stopped his pacing now and is coming towards me with the softness and sureness I'm used to. His hands twist together, his back curved a little so he's not at his greatest height. The sweetness in his eyes is disarming. But I came here today with a purpose. And nothing can stop me.

'Stop,' I say, and he pauses dutifully, but the longing on his stupid face is still clear as day.

'I'm sorry,' I tell him, and I really mean it.

I whisk up my laptop bag and backpack and turn on my heel. I run straight past my bus stop, forgetting to pause there. But home isn't far, and I can make it within an hour.

I slow down eventually, when I realise Artie isn't following me. The evening breeze is cooling, brushing against my skin, raising goosebumps. It teases the trees, making the leaves bow and flutter. I wipe tears away and straighten my shoulders.

Afternoon traffic is as outrageous as it can be in Cairns and bored drivers give me strange looks as I powerwalk by them. The pathway near home is broken, cement pieces launching up at dangerous angles. My uncle keeps putting in complaints about it, but nobody does anything to fix it. The other day I watched an old lady full on face plant and a bunch of people go running her way.

It takes me fifty-four minutes to get home and when I do my shoulders are heaving from lugging bags everywhere. I'm carrying real textbooks because it gives me a headache to read the computer screen for too long. Our school library only has a few copies of each book, and they aren't supposed to lend them out, but the librarians are nice to me. Nik reckons I need to make more friends. She was ecstatic when I started dating Artie. She reckons she finally had a real sister she could relate to.

I walk into the front yard of our house, noting my uncle's two cars are parked under the tin carport. Mum's using his dodgy second car to drive around to interviews each day and to take me and my little brother to school.

I open the door and the familiarity is a salve to my raw emotions. I can smell a stew bubbling in the kitchen as my uncle and his boyfriend stir and bicker and share a beer. Mum is in the lounge with my little brother beside her as he silently reads his book for school like he does every afternoon. They struggle through his homework each day. Nik is on her phone, bright makeup a beacon to my eyes. And my grandparents are sitting in the lounge chairs, tea in their hands as they watch Neighbours.

I sit down on the big couch on Mum's other side and lay my head against her shoulder. I don't say anything about the breakup yet. I don't say anything beyond a hello. They know I'm not much of a talker. I watch as people on the soap opera mess up, again and again. But the characters move through time differently — a half hour episode can contain massive amounts of unrealistic drama. Forgiveness is a plot tool, something to move one character on to another story line. It doesn't always make sense and my Aka and Mum always point at the TV and claim 'fake' when it happens. In my family, love is endless. Forgiveness is not.

Don't date stupid or dangerous people.

I take out my phone and bring up Artie's name.

DIS/SIMULATION

AÏSHA TRAMBAS

ii. the set up

listen.

if you hadn't already heard about ancestor simulation theory, then buckle up and hold on, because this one took me a lil minute to wrap my head around. unsure whether it was my lack of mathematical and physics reasoning skills that prevented this scientific theory from 'clicking' sooner, or more so the deep inward unrest at the whiteness of it all!

imagine needing a PhD in philosophy, several (astro) physics, computing, and neuroscience degrees, complex mathematical calculations, and an imagination bent on expanding planetary extraction of galactic resources… all to simply theorise a future in which humans take mass interest in engaging with the realities, minds and experiences of their ancestors.

i'm rushing ahead. let me try my hardest at linearity for just one moment, because i promise you i don't have more of it to give than that.

"unless we are now living in a simulation, our descendants will almost certainly never run an ancestor simulation."

this quote is lifted from nick bostrom, a swedish-born oxford university physicist, philosopher and polymath. it is pulled from his 2003 research paper titled, 'are we living in a computer simulation?'[i] in this paper, bostrom puts forward an argument for the possibility of what he terms: 'the ancestor simulation'.

'the ancestor simulation' involves a scenario in which future descendants of our current human species reach a point of such technological advancement that they can simulate the realities and experiences of every human mind who had ever lived before them, several times over. such a computational project would theoretically require the ability to convert the energy of entire planets into computers, generating a simulation capacious enough to easily mimic the trillions of synaptic pathways in the average human brain. our future descendants could thus, hypothetically, imitate our present environment in high enough fidelity as to be indistinguishable from reality to the minds existing within the simulation itself:

AKA, the ancestors of the descendants.

AKA, us?

according to bostrom — and sketched here by your resident non-physicist and year 9 STEM drop-out — the ancestor simulation is of course not the *only* possibility. it is possible that human populations never reach this enormous computational capacity and are therefore unable to run such a simulation; *or* that even if they did acquire the means, that there could simply be a lack of interest or purpose for such a metaphysical exercise in future human civilisations.

if the first option *were* accurate, that our descendants *did* decide to initiate an ancestor simulation, then this would have enormous repercussions for our contemporary understanding of reality, and this, i believe, is the significance and possibility at the heart of bostrum's inquiry. crucially, he argues that in terms of sheer mathematical probability (and *don't* ask me about that part), in a post-ancestor simulation world, the simulated minds would far outnumber any original human minds, and thus any given consciousness in existence by that stage would far likelier be a result of the simulation, rather than an original human mind.

this game of probability is what allows bostrum to conclude that: unless we are — right now — living in that very simulation, our descendants will almost certainly never run one.

i think about ancestor simulation theory a lot these days. it bleeds naturally into the well-worn synaptic pathways inside me, tracing the spiritual bankruptcy of whiteness with diurnal regularity, seeking to understand. what exactly? i'm not sure. can't be anything good to be gleaned, but there might be some truths.

i wonder, could this be a(nother) case of whiteness compensating for its metaphysical deadness with calculated numerical probabilities? theorising one's descendants' future roles and responsibilities for parallel world-building, rather than taking up one's own forebears about their responsibilities regarding *this* world?

when i die, it is not my hope that my far descendants can ever simulate me. it is my hope that they never need to. wanting, for them, every effort against dis/simulation.

iv. what i heard

to tell you about what they said
i would need another language,
of light on the inside, another
lesson in how to receive lessons, just so:

sun giving reprieve from cloud,
totalising your bedroom,
flooded
at the peak of prayer.

a   light   swells   over
the names of your dead,
and the unknown ones,
with precision.

they said i would need another language
to tell you   *about what?*

only got what i heard and conferred with Spirit,
shared, breathed and beed. seed
that wind carried truth,
and though i am air, am not wind,
but wanting wind's voice[ii].

we am not wind, but mistaken for weightless,
the way we were
reduced to no matter at all,
or to the question of it.

we am wind's voice, singing
proof of the infinite,
infinitesimal unseen.

to tell you
about
that holy mass,
we use another language.

i. the word, convicted

the word *convicted*, sighed or exclaimed
intonation of pentecostal church people
plummets
    that which is breathed or blown

        (pneuma)
      down
        my
        spine
      all shades
     of relief,
    release
  and
    surrender.

i am convicted.

no take-backs but traced back
to understand, underhand latin
euphemisms, 'to fight and conquer',
then 'to overcome by argument',
then 'to convince of wrongdoing or
sin', etymologically.
this language is full to breaking,
with   the stench   of
dom-   i-   nation

in
diaphanous silks
speaking dissimulation[iii].

i bought my uncle a brick
for christmas, in 2006.
i was ten.
it was an inside joke.
he laughed.
and i was smug.

ten dollars worth of
    pocket money,
    and a trip out to richmond
ten dollars worth of
    ye olde ~ convict labour ~
ten dollars worth of
    land theft wrapped in newspaper,
    sold roadside off sandstone strips of
    ~ heritage ~.

is it too aspirational?
from 2006, buying convict bricks
now to wish: a legacy, a leaving,
descendants with some
meagre minutiae

of the inside/outside colony
d i s m e m b e r e d.

i *am convicted.*

iii. what we said

a lot about memory and the lack of. about the humpty
dumpty of trauma and family and working our ways up to
a stunning kintsugi one day, maybe. a lot about apocalypse
prep and running out of air and water and life. a lot about
what required destruction and deconstruction, about what
to create, and what about where we were ever going to find
the energy and expertise for all that?
(answer: practice). a lot about how we couldn't wait to stop
lying to ourselves but got right up and continued to as if
other people's lies were a matter of our survival and not
another way around: our survival being the matter of other
people's lies.

about: how at some point (yesterday!) we needed to
          prepare for the end of the internet and phones.
about: flying out to return to else-wheres where, perhaps,
          we weren't as welcome or useful as we wanted to be.
          (we still wanted to be elsewhere, go [redacted]).
about: "sometimes i can't tell which thoughts are just

thoughts, and which thoughts are actually
anc*st*rs talking."

about: "such as?"

about: "i keep hearing the words [redacted]. but like, on
repeat."

about: "nah sis, that one's definitely anc*st*rs."

about: forgetting how to hear the the mercy in the wind
and trees warning us, over plastic-wrapped picnic
conversations.

about: how long it would take for us little city people to
cark it, giving our best crack at subsistence
agriculture and communalism.

about: what it feels like standing at the border of: we-
will-never-not-use-humour-to-cope, and, the-
stakes-have-become-un-laughable.

we were as prepared as we could have been, but not as we'd
hoped to be.

v. safekeeping dream AKA
what we re-membered

luscious-hearted people sustain
me.

i am

on a ground of some kind
rolling forehead to floor in the shape of
infinity.

i am
safekept
if only in believing so.

[i] nick bostrom, 'Are We Living in a Computer Simulation?', *The Philosophical Quarterly*, Vol 53. No. 211, 2003. https://www.simulation-argument.com/simulation.pdf.

[ii] audre lorde, 'Bloodbirth', *Cables to Rage*, 1970.

[iii] "Dissimulation makes us dysfunctional since it encourages us to deny what we genuinely feel and experience, we lose our capacity to know who we really are and what we need and desire." in bell hooks', *Sisters of the Yam: Black Women and Self-Recovery*, 1993, p. 24.

History Repeating

LISA FULLER

It's all one big web granddaughter. If you try to ignore it, you'll get tangled up.

They march us out of the elevator towards the world's worst carnival ride. The pre-dawn light glints off the metal structure, filtering slowly through the scaffolding around us. A new day, the chill air nipping at my ears and nose. It should've felt promising. Instead, it pokes thousands of holes through my clothing.

We stand in a tight cluster like a herd of frightened cattle, our backs against the rails of the walkway. Watching, waiting. The material of the strange black jumpsuits they'd forced us into is itchy sandpaper against my chilled skin. My limbs tremble from lack of food or water. But the grip on my sister's hand is strong.

'Form an ordered line,' a uniform barks. 'Number 1 to the front.'

He points at the gaping door at the end of the scaffold. Out of the yawning deep a woman in a white coat appears like a reverse ghost. Her cheery wave makes me want to swear at her.

When no one moves, the uniform shifts his hand, fondling the butt of his weapon. A thin girl, maybe seven, shuffles past me. The masking tape stuck to the top left corner of her chest bears a simple 'R1' in permanent marker. She's so tiny she barely reaches my ribs.

Slowly, the next numbers follow. I count them. Before staring down at the 'R49' on my breast, and the 'R35' on Edie's. I'll be second last in line, the order based on height or age, I wasn't sure. It's hard to uncurl my fingers from my sister's, but I force myself to do it. Willing away tears and shushing her softly, I point to the girl with 'R34', gesturing for her to follow, before shuffling backwards to make room.

They unloaded us an hour before. Right after we finished changing in full view of each other and everyone outside the windows. Shameless eyes watched us, as we crawled out of our pyjamas, or whatever we'd been wearing when they'd come. I wished so hard I could do the same with my skin. The jumpsuits were utilitarian, nothing on them at all but a front zipper. The boots were slightly hardier, but not by much.

As we exited the train carriages the soldiers were everywhere, collecting their carriage kids like bizarre black swans grabbing orphaned cygnets. I cast my eyes around, trying to see any adults in the sea of children and youth. No one but the uniforms, and none that I recognised. It was almost a relief.

A single person in white stood on a stool, pointing first in one direction, then another.

The uniform who loved to grope his weapon had waved us along. Rough pushes and cursing were the response for anyone who dared pause. Country help you if you asked a question or made a noise.

It's why we're all silent on the scaffolding. The odd sniff of a snotty nose rasps softly.

R1 reaches the portal and the woman in white steps back. R1 glances back at us all. I give her the 'hurry up' chin flick, but not fast enough. A rough hand lands on her back, shoving her through. I wince at the thud. Anger making my fists curl tight. She was only a kid for fuck's sake.

But so was I.

Once I'd have fought anyone who said that. I'd have argued till I was blue in the face: *I'm grown. A teenager now.* I'd snuck out to a party that night. Was it only three years ago?

My best friend, Katie, had picked me up and we'd driven out to the river. Music floated across the night sky, someone brought beers. My boyfriend Chris had wrapped me up in his strong arms and we'd snuck off away from the firelight. A few short minutes later, a yell of panic brought us back.

'Did you see?' One of the girls was waving a phone around.

The screen lit up showing the new regime. The ones no one thought would win. Their banners of nationalism, faith and hope. Not too bad surely?

A small change, they said. Only four years.

They hadn't needed that long.

Year one Chris had stopped being my boyfriend. He blamed his parents, but I saw fear in his eyes when he looked at me, and worse. Year two the school had sent out an email, requesting we not attend. Anyone of our 'type' was better off home-schooled. For their own safety.

Protection. That hated word.

This year it became 'safer to stay home' and not go out unless we had to. My friends had still visited for a while, slowly tapering away till even Katie stopped answering my texts.

Staring at the blank faces of the few uniforms around me, I'd never wanted to be a kid again so badly.

Last month I'd heard Mum and Dad whispering in their bedroom. About going bush. I'd barged in and begged them not to. I couldn't imagine my life without phones, wifi, electricity, indoor plumbing! Chris would come around, so would Katie and the others. We just had to hang in there, the regime would be voted out and it would all go back to normal. Everyone said so.

If only I had let us run, would we be loaded up in the trucks still? I hadn't seen my parents in three days, and it was my fault.

Three days on a suffocating carriage filled to the brim with bodies, ranging in age from five to just shy of eighteen. No adults.

Twice a day carts rolled through with 'food' that smelled rancid. A single toilet at the back got clogged on day one. After that I didn't let Edie or myself eat.

No one spoke much. We'd formed little clusters in the threadbare seats. Three or four sometimes cramming into two seats. Brothers and sisters, maybe cousins. The crying was sporadic, bouts coming from different directions. Most of it soft. We knew no one would come wipe our tears. I held on to Edie and prayed to anyone that would listen.

Fear will get ya every time bub, it's what makes em do this now. But fear ain't all bad neither. Ya can't be brave if ya aren't scared.

I stare up at the huge contraption. Dreading its circular shining skin. A giant metal tampon to soak up blood. Disposal.

Stepping closer, I enter the behemoth's shadow and feel the weight. A cold shiver races down my spine.

Nan would say it was a sign. One that said I should run.

I send out another prayer that her and Gramps, and all the old aunties and uncles are okay. We hadn't known to say goodbye. They'd rolled into our yard in the middle of the night. These strangers with their dark uniforms, military like, blunt and to the point.

No one would answer Dad's questions or Mum's demands. We weren't allowed to take anything, not even our wallets or phones. My parents stopped asking questions then, bundling us up in jumpers and taking us outside to the truck. Looking up into that flat tray with the high wire on all sides, I was horrified and relieved to see Nan and Gramps waiting. Pulling us up into their arms.

Arriving at the train station, we were unloaded onto a packed platform. People were pushing, shoving, screaming, crying. Some were from our town, other faces I recognised from dispersed smaller communities.

The bright fluorescent lights finally showed me the uniforms' faces. These were people I'd grown up with, been taught by, worked for over the school holidays. They looked at us like we were animals in a sale yard now.

Mum kept calling out the names of her aunties and uncles, siblings and their children. But no one could hear her above the noise.

She held me and Edie under her arms, Dad kept hold of Nan and Gramps. His mob were two hours away, they wouldn't be here. I could see his fears by the strain of his knuckles.

A man in white had stood up on something with a bullhorn, 'Property of East State High School' on the side.

'Quiet now everyone, just quiet down.'

People yelled louder, finding a face to vent their fear at.

A gun shot stopped everything.

I don't remember much after that. My heart was pounding too loud in my chest.

At some point, uniforms wove through the groups, pushing and shoving. The 18 to 60-year-old men were weeded out. Forced up to the yellow safety line. Not given time for kisses or hugs. They were culling the strongest from us.

Edie sobbed into Mum's chest as they shoved Dad on a train, words of reunion 'on the other side' ringing in our ears. The last thing Dad said was an order thrown over the shoulder of a uniform: 'Stay strong daughter, and no matter what happens, take care of your sister.'

I nodded even as I sobbed like I was younger than Edie. Even though it was all my fault as they dragged him away to the men's train. Forcing him away from us. Mum's turn came after. I was crying too hard to hear her. None of the adults cried. Nan told me once that you forget how after a while.

Then it was our turn.

Shoved onto the train, we made it to two empty seats. Edie and I stared out at our grandparents. Nan's hard face, stone-set and glaring at the uniforms. Gramps stood at her back, like always. Their train was coming too. I still wished for one more look into those powder blue eyes.

The uniforms told us we'd see them too, on the other side.

No one believed them.

They file us into their machine now, one pace forward at a time. I see Edie reach the portal, willing her not to look back. She keeps her head down, vanishing over the lip and into the dark. I want to sigh at the same time as forcing down a sob. My fault.

I stare down at my feet, the boots they'd given me are

tight and pinching. Beneath that, the steel grate let me see the processions below. More kids, all being herded into the same metal tomb.

Lifting my head, I can see more black boots above me. The elevators are spewing us out like ants.

A whack to the back of my head sends me lurching forward. My teeth clacking together. I bite my tongue, not bothering to throw a glare. We'd learned fast not to give cheek on that train ride.

Stepping up the rungs, I throw a leg up and over the entry. This close, the metal didn't gleam so much; I could see the smears and marks of rushed work. My boilermaker cousin would have sent his apprentice back to fix it up right. And this wasn't some vat that held nothing but liquid.

It took a second for my eyes to adjust to the gloom. A large circular space, with weird configurations all along the walls. Compartments and bulkheads so shadowed it was impossible to make them out. The ring of boots on yet more grates bounced off the walls, echoing back so hard it hurt. A million feet above, below, around me.

They hadn't trained us in using any of this, how the fuck did they expect us to survive?

Maybe I'd just answered my own question.

The floor was a mass of seats, laid out in concentric circles. Oysters in a can. My scanning gaze can't find Edie's curls.

'Move,' grunts a uniform, pushing me toward the white

coat, who is standing at the centre of it all.

She points at the front row, five chairs facing inwards. I step forward and sit down, trying not to react as she reaches over my body, pulling straps across and clicking them into a fixture at my belly button. She yanks three times on the belts.

I'm still craning my neck. Searching for Edie.

A sharp pinch on my shoulder and I jerk. Turning back to find the woman shoving a used needle into a pouch tied to her belt.

'What did you—'

She's already turning away to direct R50 to the last open seat across from mine.

Sweat beaded along my lip and heat flushes up my neck. I fight the animal urges, my blood racing, carrying whatever she'd just given me faster and further throughout my body.

Forcing deep breaths through my nose. Out through my mouth.

Share all your stories, what we told ya and what ya remember. And not just the brave ones, but the weak and the mistakes. Learn em. Learn from em so ya don't repeat em.

I stare around me; things are coming slower into focus. Faces.

There are no smiles, or grins. No sobs either. It's too dark to see much detail. The air feels tight, like a rubber band about to snap. I can't see the floor anymore, but above me is the same. Grates and boots.

Soft whimpers carry clearer as the stamping feet slow.

Growing higher above us.

The woman in white walks to the very centre of the space. Her hands clasped in front of her and she's grinning like a lunatic. A true believer.

'You're all set. A better world awaits you on the other side.'

'Oh yeah, want my seat?' R50 whispers. Her voice shaking and a little slurred.

A few snorts of laughter. In that metal boombox, we all heard her. And so had the white coat.

'This is for your benefit,' she tutted. 'You just don't know any better. We're saving you.'

The condescension drips and I roll my eyes. Sharing a look with R50.

'We're nothing but your fucking canaries.'

A sharp slap to my face, but somehow blurred. I hadn't even realised I'd opened my mouth.

She leans into my face then, her angelic smile morphed to malice. It's oddly terrifying to be confronted by a stranger's hate.

'So go do what all good canaries must,' she whispers to me, before standing to survey us. 'God bless you.'

She steps past me, out of sight. I can't turn my head much. The belt across my arms and torso hold me so tight to the chair I can't even gain an inch.

Below us there's a far-off boom that makes me jump.

Then another.

Closer and closer. Synchronised. Efficient.

The door to our level slams shut, making the same note. Boom.

Then the one above us, and onwards into silence. More mechanical noises sound off. Strange hisses and rumbles.

The debates about off-world deportation had begun that first year. There'd been no consultation, just a bunch of regime members pushing for 'the good'. Their eyes glazed with the certainty that they were right, and holy. Zealots, Mum had spat.

It had always felt far off. Unreal. Who would let that happen?

'Dani,' a voice whispers from behind me, breaching the pain that threatens to swallow me.

On instinct I try to look, but I'm stuck. I want to panic, rip at the straps and just lose my ever-loving shit.

But I breathe through it. I'd promised Dad. Not like a 'I won't sneak out any more promise' either. Maybe my last one to him.

I work my arm backward, extending my shoulder till it hurts, stretching a hand out.

Soft gloved fingers find mine. Intertwining.

I want to open my mouth. Say something to help. But what could ever help this?

My eyes meet the girl across from me. The cheeky one from before. I see my own pain and fear reflected.

Anger is a start, granddaughter, but it'll only take you so far before it destroys you. Hope will carry you through to the end. Hope and each other.

Gramps' final words to us. He whispered them after they took Mum. Pulling our arms from around him and Nan, he wrapped me and Edie up in each other. Placing our palms together till our fingers interlocked.

This isn't about just me. Not anymore. My jaw hardens and I set my spine, just like Nan on that cursed platform.

I open my mouth and say loudly, 'We're going to be okay. We're in this together, no matter what.'

Not profound. Not deep. Just certain. My eyes met those I could see. A weird calm descends. I reach my right hand out to the girl beside me. Her hand grips mine and I see some of her panic fade. Hands reach out in all directions. I hear it more than I see it.

'We're sisters now,' I promise. Nods answer me.

A roaring starts far below, building higher. Drowning out any other sound. Then the shaking hit, rattling my teeth. I wonder if the engines will tear us apart before we even leave the atmosphere.

I look around at those in my circle. At least one of the faces has their mouth wide open and screaming. But I can't hear them. Hands stay gripping tight. The roar eats everything. Pressure tight on my eardrums.

R50 looks across at me, yells something. I choke in a breath. Remembering to breathe.

Whatever she'd shot us up with was slowly dragging me

under. Lulling my mind into an ease I hadn't felt since that party three years ago.

The seats jerk, flipping backwards so we're horizontal, facing the sky and the rows and rows of people above us. Forcing our hands to drop, but not the connection. I feel too muddled to react, but the loss of Edie's hand hurts. A great force throws me back, pressing hard on my chest as the silver coffin lifts. Pushing against the planet's gravity.

Our planet. But no more.

So said the white coats.

The four-year change would come too late for us.

*

We lost a lot of people in the crossing. Even more grieved themselves to death after we landed. For family, for Country. The severing too great a pain for them to bear.

For those of us who made it? We remembered. We survived. And eventually, we thrived. Together.

White Dunes

AFEIF ISMAIL

CO-TRANSCREATED FROM ARABIC
BY DR VIVIENNE GLANCE AND AFEIF ISMAIL

She does not come as they had agreed. He decides not to
wait, as is his habit since he fell in love with her. He locks
the door of his isolated room in the far corner of the house.
Twice he makes sure he has locked the metal windows,
then he pushes his wardrobe in front of the door. He writes
a short letter and puts it on the table beside his bed. He
unwraps a sharp razor blade and without any hesitation he
cuts the veins of his wrist, then lies down on the bed directly
beneath the rotating ceiling fan. Calmly he contemplates it
without any fear as it moves slowly above him. At first, the
blood pumps quickly and then it starts to slow down, drop
by drop and he begins to feel unable to control his body. He
tries to match his breath as much as he can to the rhythm of
his heartbeat as it gradually weakens.

He feels a sharp pain in his heart as he remembers his

childhood friend shouting for him to swim in the River Nile. Teasing, laughing loudly and calling him a coward, his friend splashed him with water. He hid his anger and turned his head to watch a hopping frog nearby and he wished that his friend would drown. He distracted himself by throwing stones into the water, sitting near his friend's luxurious, imported clothes. He cast his fishing line hoping to catch a fish large enough to feed his three young brothers. Then he gazed far away watching a bird feed her chicks. He did not hear his friend's three intermittent screams. When he turned his head he saw bubbles boiling the surface of the water, then becoming a large circle. He was confused. He did not know what to do. Quickly, he grabbed his friend's luxurious clothes and ran to his friend's house, leaving them at the front gate, which was newly decorated. He disappeared before anyone noticed him.

He is panting hard when he feels a sharp, burning pain coming from his wrist. He turns his head to the wall through which he used to hear his parents fighting, even though his room was far from the rest of the house. He remembers his mother complaining when his father became drunk every day, that they did not have anything to feed the children because he spent all their money on his lying illusion, increasing his misery; his father screaming, shouting, damning all women-kind without exception, even his own mother, who brought him into this world. He hears him slapping her face and calling her a bitch and saying,

- The bird wakes every day at dawn, hungry, and it doesn't know its fortune. But then it comes back in the evening, singing, with a full stomach — and it has some to feed its chicks as well!

He feels a delicious numbness invading his pores. He remembers a melody from his childhood, played by a goatherd. It echoed with the continuous sighing of his breath, as he blew through the mouthpiece of his single-holed, homemade flute. He breathed out all his primitive pain and his inherited sadness, from generation to generation, grandfather to father, their only profession to run after these crazy creatures, which never stay in rhythm. He smiles when he recalls the goats returning in the evening, scratching against their mud house until they wore away a curve. After all his father's useless attempts to paint it with discarded sump oil and petrol, still the goats only knew that craving desire to scratch their skin on the wall.

He feels his throat drying and twice tries to swallow his saliva.

The great desert was in front of them without any borders after their car broke down travelling to Libya. The confident driver promised them they were going to drink tea that morning in Tripoli. Because of their ignorance of geography, they believed him and paid the full fee without discount. All their provisions and water were only enough for half a day. Why would they need dried food? They were sure they were only hours from a green Eden that would feed them with a delicious meal as described by their relatives, who had lived there for many years. As the second day passed, all of them were exhausted except the driver's assistant who sang rude songs whilst he helped the driver without any sign of tiredness. Patiently, he accepted the curses from the driver when he ordered him to climb on top of the car to bring down some heavy bags, or when told to lie down on the burning sand on a day without shadows, to change a small part. All the passengers thought the assistant, with his singing and high energy, must have a secret store of water and food. When he walked away to relieve himself, in a flash he found more than ten hands grabbing the small cup he was urinating into. The smelly liquid splashed all over their clothes and they still quarreled, while the driver's assistant stood, astonished, with his pants below his knees.

A slight headache, like a burning pulse, is pounding on the left side of his head. She did not come as they had agreed! Where is she now? She may be doing what they had agreed upon alone in another place, so as not to break his heart by bleeding in front of him. It might be she crossed over before him and is already waiting for him. What a kind gentle soul she is, as if descended from weightless phantoms. She does not belong to this life, which is like a congested nose you need to blow as quickly as you can. Maybe she has changed her mind, like last time!

He starts to smell the blood with all of his senses. He thinks he might have slept a little, and he fights the desire to scream for help, but at the same time not wanting to. When he finally decides to scream, his voice drowns in the passage of a nightmarish labyrinth. There is no echo outside his soul. He opens his eyes widely; he only sees a white colour spreading whenever he looks deeper into it. He thinks it might be a trick of his eyes due to the tiredness of his mind. When he tries to touch his bleeding veins he only touches a white feeling. He turns his head in all directions but what he can see is only dunes of white in front of him, even when he tries to look beyond them. When he looks at the ceiling, he finds it has become white, without any borders. At that point he understands he is only part of a luminous scattering of whiteness sleeping like a distant light.

He realises he is flying near a white cloud. When he looks left and right he sees tens of lilywhite birds carrying him, lullabying him with their floating wings and lovely tunes. He becomes weightless, just sleeping light. The leader of the majestic flock is two wingspans ahead of the group, her neck coloured in two bands of blue and yellow and the rest of her body a light green except for the tail, which is patterned with the same colours as her neck. When she tweets, all the whiteness wakes from its sleep and shapes start to come back to things, as if her majestic tweet is the breath of life. A flowering garden wakes with blossoms and aroma; even lovers are hugging each other in adoration like a prayer, embracing each other with never-ending kisses; the shiny stones in the passage glow. At first, he thinks they might have been brought from the banks of the Red Sea, but when he looks closely at them he finds they are blocks of diamonds and alabaster, each shaped a similar geometric size. A fountain splashes perfumes he has never smelt before, its aromas spreading in all directions. The bird with the coloured neckbands tweets one long note, and in front of him the Nile appears with green banks and soft golden sand. He gazes at the riverbed and sees every coloured creature swimming as if they were reflected in a mirror. He sees on the riverbed his childhood friend smiling, playing and calling for him to join him. He shivers like light when he realises that his friend is swimming in the same clothes he had left at the front gate. For more than twenty years, he has not been able to face his friend's mother, and his friend's picture is embroidered into his memory; everyday he replays it over and over for hours, and this has made all the people around him avoid sitting with his castle of silence made from pain and memory. They left him alone with his fractured mind. When he spoke he only had one favourite topic: his drowning, childhood friend, as if the train of life had stopped at that station ever since he had gone.

The leading bird tweets again and from the womb of the whiteness appears a small, royal boat that can only carry two people. The majestic flock carries him to the boat. The waves do not break as it moves even though there are no oars or any motor or any source of energy. The boat sails against the current of the river without the water rippling, as if it is moving on transparent ice. His friend, wearing the clothes that he had left in front of the house, follows them from below the surface like a young, playful dolphin, and he is followed by all the Nile creatures imitating the movements of his hands and short legs. It has become like a huge orchestra playing with harmony, playing a lovely tune that they all know by heart. Whenever they go deeper and deeper into the river, the tweeting from the bird of life becomes higher and higher and more continuous. On the bank of the river grows an equatorial forest of mango trees full of purple coloured fruit. Above this, winged horses fly like flashing fire, their tails and manes expand resembling a flock of peacocks. Behind them a herd of elephants are wearing the shirt of the zebra, their tusks made of ebony. A black giraffe tries to reach the branches of the papaya trees planted in the air. Racing crocodiles, the size of dinosaurs, pass. The air drizzles with a lovely perfume he has never smelt before. It drops onto the ground and splashes the perfume fountain. From it, transparent bubbles form and inside each is a brown child with cupid features. Phantoms of drunken souls try to pop the bubbles to reincarnate the children's souls, but the playful bubbles make a game of their jumping and float higher and higher, escaping their grasp and leaving those drunken souls wandering and stranded on a level they cannot go above. They return full of disappointment and sit upon droplets of dew on the petals of a Thai rose.

Suddenly, fireworks explode in the sky and from this

emerges Mexican singers with guitars. They stay in the air before a big white cloud engulfs them. When the bird of life stops her exquisite melody and fearfully turns to him, she points to the huge white cloud a feather-distance away, just about to engulf her. She points to his drowning friend, which the spectacle had distracted him from. He is now struggling for breath and calls for him to save him. He looks into the eyes of the bird of life just as the whiteness starts to engulf her, leaving only her banded blue and yellow neck. He is surprised to discover that her eyes are the same eyes as his lover who didn't come at the time they had agreed. When he sees the fear in her eyes, he knows she did not break her promise. He turns his head to his drowning friend, determined this time to save him, but he finds the river has become a vast landscape of white dunes.

كُثبَان بَيْضَاء*

عفيف إسماعيل

لم تأتِ كما اتَّفَقا!، فقرَّر ألا يَنتظِرَها كما هي عادته منذ أن أحبَّها. أحكَم إغلاقَ باب غرفته المعزولة في ركنٍ بعيدٍ عن بقية غُرَف المنزل، تأكَّدَ مرتين من أنه أغلق كل الشبابيك الحديديّة جيداً، حرّكَ دولاب ملابسه ووَضَعَه أمام باب الغرفة. كتَب رسالةً قصيرةً ووَضَعها على المنضدة أمامه، ثمّ فضَّ غلاف شفرة الحلاقة الحادّة، وبلا ترددُ قطَع شرايين رسْغ يده اليسرى، ثمّ استلقى على السّرير الذي أعدّه لحصُوصاً لهذه المهمة، إذ وَضَعَهُ تحت مروحة السقف التي تدور ببطءٍ، وهو يتأمّلها بهدوءٍ لا رهبة فيه. تساقطت قطرات الدّم بغزارة في البداية، ثمّ قليلاً... قليلاً أخذت تُبطئ، وبدأ يَفقد السيطرة على جسده، حاوَل أن يتحكَّم في أنفاسه بقدْر المستطاع؛ أن يَجعلها مُنتظمةً مع دقّات قلبه التي بدأ الوهن يَدبُّ فيها رُويداً... رُويداً.

أَحَسَّ بوجع طفيفٍ في قلبه حين تذكَّر صديق طفولته الوحيد وهو يدعوه إلى السباحة معه في النيل، ويَصِفُه بالجُبن، ويُلاحقه بقهقهاته الساخرة ورشقات الماء. أخْفى حنقه عنه والتفتَ يَرمُق ضفدعةً تتقافز قُربه، وتَمنَّى له الغَرَق!، ثمّ انشغَلَ عنه بِرَمْي الحصى على سطح الموج وهو يجلس على الضفّة إلى جانب ملابس صديقه المستوردة الزاهيّة المكوّمة أمامه. رَمَى سنّارته في الماء عسى أن تصطاد له سمكةً كبيرةً تكفي وجبةً له وإخوته الثلاثة الصغار، ثم حدَّق بعيداً خلف طائرٍ يُطعم صغاره. لم يَنتبه إلى صرخات صديقه الثلاث المتقطِّعة، وعندما التفتَ رأى فقاقيعَ تفور، ثم تَكبُر دوائرُها. ارتبك. لم يَدْرِ ما يفعل. ركض مُسرعاً وحَمَل الملابس الفاخرة إلى بيت صديقه ووَضَعَها أمام الباب المزخرف بنقوشٍ جديدةٍ الطِّلاء، واختفى قبل أن يَرَاه أحد.

تلاحقَت أنفاسُه سريعاً، حين أحسَّ حارقي بوَخزٍ حارقٍ عند رسْغ يده اليسرى، فالتفتَ إلى الحائط المقابل الذي يتسرَّب منه يوميّاً، برغم ابتعاده عن غرف المنزل الأخرى، شِجَار أمّه وأبيه ليلاً عندما يعود أبوه محموراً، إذ تُذَكِّره بأن ليس لديهم ما يَسُدُّ الرَّمَق ليوم غَدٍ، لماذا يُهْدِر كلّ ما تبقّى لديهم خلف هذا الوهم الكاذب الذي يَزيد من تعاستهما. يَلعن أبوه، بصوته المشروخ، كلَّ النساء، ولا يَستثني منهن حتى أمّه التي جاءت به إلى هذا العالم!، ويَنتهرها بقسوة، ثم يَصفعها، ويَصفها بالفاجرة، ثم يقول له:

. إنّ الطير يَخرج كلّ صباحٍ جائعاً، ولا يَعْلَم رزقه، ويَعود مُمتلئ البطن يُغنّي كما كان يغنّي قبل قليل ومعه زادُ صغاره.

يُحِسُّ بِخدرٍ لذيذٍ يَغزو مَسامه. يتذكّر معزوفةً موسيقيةً، سَمعها من راعي الأغنام في طفولته البعيدة، تتردّد بزفيرٍ مُتلاحقٍ، يَنفخه من فُوَّهة مزماره ذي الثقبِ الواحدِ الذي صَنَعه بنفسه، ليزفِرَ فيه أوجاعَه البدائيّةَ وحُزناً مُتوارثاً منذ أجيالٍ، أباً عن جدٍّ، كلَّهم يَمتهنون السَّعيَ خلف المخلوقات المجنونة التي لا ضابط لها. ابتسَمَ وهو يَرى الأغنامَ، في أوَيَتِها المسائيّة، تَحتكُّ بحائط منزلهم الطينيّ وتَنحرُهُ من وسطه، بعد أن فشلت كلُّ محاولات أبيه اليائسة بدهنه بمخلَّفات زيوت العربات مخلوطةً ببعض الشحوم البتروليّة؛ لكن الأغنام لا تعترف بغير تلك الرغبة الحارقة في أن تَحُكَّ جلدَها بهذا الحائط.

يُحِسُّ بجفافٍ حَلْقِه، يَردّد لعابُه مرّتين. الصحراءُ الكُبرى أمامهم تبدو بلا حدود، بعد أن تعطّلت العربة التي تُقلُّهم إلى ليبيا. سائقها، من فَرْط الثقة، وَعَدَهم بأن يشربوا شاي الصباح في طرابلس، ولجهلِهم بجغرافيا المنطقة صَدَّقوه، ونَقدوه ما اتفقوا عليه بلا نقصان. لم يكن ما يحملون جميعاً من زادٍ وماءٍ يكفي نصفَ يوم. لماذا يحتاجون الطعام اليابس؟، وهم على يقينٍ من أنهم على مرمى ساعاتٍ من جنةٍ خضراء سوف تُطعمهم بما لَذّ وطاب؛ كما وَصَفَها العائدون منها الذين عاشوا بها سنيناً عددا. ها هو اليوم الثاني يَمرُّ، والإعياء الثقيل يُصيب الجميع، عدا مساعد السائق الذي ما زال يَترنّم بالأغنيات الخليجية، وهو يعاون السائق بلا كَلَلٍ، مُحتمِلاً لعناتِه التي يَصُبُّها عليه بين كل لحظةٍ وأخرى، ويأمرُه أن يصعد سريعاً إلى سطح العربة الحارق ليُخفِّف حمولة العربة من الأثقال التي تُحمِّلها، أو أن يرقد تحت العربة، ومن تحته صهدُ جَمرٍ تحار لا ظِلَّ فيه، كي يربط قطعة غبار صغيرة. ظلَّ الجميعُ أن مساعد السائق، المتدفِّق حيويةً، والذي لم يتوقّف عن الغناء، يُخفي طعاماً وماءً في مكانٍ ما. عندما ذهب ليُقضي حاجتَه بعيداً عنهم، بعد أقلَّ من لحظةٍ وهو يتبوّل في كوبٍ صغيرٍ، وَجَدَ أباً كثيرةً تَتخطّفُه، ويتدفّق السائل ذو الرائحة الثاقبة بين ملابسهم وهم يتعاركون، بينما مساعد السائق يَقِف مبهوتاً وسرواله تحت ركبتيه.

دُوارٌ خفيفٌ، وصُداعٌ مثل نبضٍ حارقٍ يَنبض في الجهة اليسرى من رأسه. لم تأتِ كما اتفقا، أين هي الآن؟ لعلَّها تُنفِّذ ما اتَّفقا عليه وحدَها في مكانٍ ما، حتى لا تُوجِع قلبَه بدَمِها النازف أمامه، لعلَّها عَبَرَت قبلَه، وتَنظرُه هناااااااااك!. يا لها من حانيةٍ من نَسلِ الرَّهافةِ والطَّيفِ، لا تَنتمي إلى هذه الحياةِ التي تُشبِهُ احتقاناً في الأنفِ لا بُدَّ من التخلُّص منه سريعاً وبأي وسيلة. أتكونُ قد تراجعت كما فعلَتْها في المرة السابقة!؟.

بدأ يَشُمُّ رائحة الدَّم تُحاصر كلَّ حواسّه. ظنَّ أنه غفا قليلاً، وهو يغالب رغبةً حارقةً في أن يَصرخ ويَطلب النجدة، غاص صوته في بجاويف عديدةٍ مثل متاهةٍ كابوسيّة، ولم يتردَّد لها أيُّ صَدًى خارجها، ففتَحَ عينيه على اتِّساعهما، لم يَجد أمامه سوى لونٍ أبيضَ يتَّسع كلّما حَدَّق في عُمقه، ظنَّ أنها إحدى خِدَع البصر، وأنَّ الوَهَن

أصابَ ذهنَه، لكنه عندما حاول أن يتحسّس شرايين يده النازفة، لم يُمسك إلا بملمسٍ أبيض، تلفّتَ في الجهاتِ فلم يَرَ سوى تلالٍ من البياض أمامه تتكثّف كلّما حاول أن يُحدّق في ما وراءها. عندما حاول أن يُحدّق نحو السقف؛ وجد أنه صار أبيض بلا حدود، أدركَ أنه لم يَعُد سوى بعضٍ من نَثراتٍ مضيئةٍ من هذا البياض، مثلما يَنام الضَّوءُ بعيداً.

انتبّه إلى أنه يَطير قربَ سحابةٍ بيضاء. عندما التفتَ يميناً ويساراً وَجد عشراتٍ من العصافير النوريّة تَحمله وتَحفُّ به وتَرفّهُ برفيفها الفاتن وغنائها النحيل. لقد صار بلا وزن؛ مَحضَ ضَوءٍ نائم!. تَطيرُ قائدةُ السِّرب الجليل على مسافةٍ جناحين في مُقدّمة الجوقة، تُزيّن رقبتها لحُزوزٌ زرقاءُ وصفراء، بينما بقيةُ ريشِها ذاتُ لونٍ أخضرَ فاقعٍ، عدا الذَّبل الذي تَخَلّى، في سيميتريّةٍ دقيقةٍ، من لونَيْ لحُزوز الرقبة، وما إنْ تُطلق تغريداتَها حتى يَصحو البياضُ المهيمنُ من غفوته، ويَعود لكلّ الأشياءِ رَونقُها، كأنّ تغريداتِها النورانيّةَ هي أنفاسُ الحياة. استفاقت أمامَه حديقةٌ كاملةٌ، مَزهُوَّة بزهورها وأريجها وفراشاتها وعُشّاقها المتعانقين في صلاةٍ عشقيّةٍ يتبادلون قُبَلاً لا تنتهي. حَصّى الممرّات مصقولٌ يَتلامَع، حتى ظَنّ في البدء أنه جُلبَ لحصُوصاً من سواحل البحر الأحمر، لكنه عندما دَقّق النظر فيه وجده بلّورات صغيرة من الماس والمرمر قُطِعَت في أشكالٍ هندسيّةٍ متساوية. النوافير تَضُخُّ عُطوراً لم يَشمّها من قبل، وعبقها يَرشح في كلّ الجهات.

أطلقت العصفورة ذات الحُروز الزرقاء والصفراء على رقبتها تغريدةً طويلةً، فتَمدّد أمامه هرٌّ بضفافٍ خضراءَ، ورملٍ ذهبيّ ناعم، حَدّقَ في عُمقِه الذي يَشفُّ عن كلّ كائناته الملوّنة مثل مرايا، في القاع رأى صديقَهُ الصّغيرَ الغارقَ مُبتسماً يَلهو، ويُشيرُ إليه لِينضمّ إليهم، ارتعَدَ كما البرق حين تَبيّن له أنّه يَسبح بكامل ملابسه تلك التي وَضعها أمام باب بيتهم؛ لم يَقْوَ على مواجهة أمّه بعدها لمدة تجاوزت العشرين عاماً لم تَغِب أبداً فيها صورته من ذاكرته!، بل تتكرّر بإلحاح فلا يُفكّر في ما عداها لساعاتٍ طويلة، مما جعل كلّ المحيطين به يتجنّبون الجلوسَ إلى صمته المُحصّن بقلاع من الأوجاع والذكريات. وتركوه وحيداً تفترسُهُ أشتاتُ ذهنه، وحتى عندما ينطق بحرف، لا يَتحدّث إلا عن صديقِه الغارق، كأنّ قطارَ الحياة توقّف به في محطّةٍ رحيله.

غَرّدَت العصفورة القائدة مرةً أخرى، فخرج من رَحِم البياض قاربٌ مُلوكيٌّ صغيرٌ لا يَسعُ أكثر من شخصين، حَمَلته العصافير النوريّة إليه. لم تتكسّر الأمواج عندما تحرّك بينها بقوة دفع لم يَعرف مصدرها!، ليس هناك مجداف أو مُحرّك أو أي طاقةٍ يعرفها. ظَلّ القارب يَمضي إلى الوراء عكس انحدار النهر، ودون أن تَحتاج المياه حوله؛ كأنّه يَسيرُ على طريقٍ مرصوفٍ بالثلج الشُّفّاف، وصديقُهُ، بكامل ملابسه التي وَضَعَها أمام بيته ذاتَ خوفٍ، يَتبعه مُبتهجاً

مثل دولفينِ صغير، وخلفه كلّ كائنات النهر تُقلّد حركات ذراعيه ورجليه الصغيرتين بين المياه، فصاروا أشبَة بأوركسترا عُظمَى تَعزف بانسجام لحناً واحداً مُتفقاً عليه بينهم.

كلّما أوغلَ في النّهر يعلو تغريد عصفورة الحياة، فتَنبُت على ضفافه غاباتٌ استوائيّة. أشجارُ مانجو مُحمّلةٌ بثمارٍ بنفسجيّة. ومن فوقها تطير خيولٌ مُجنّحةٌ كشُهبٍ ناريّة، ذيولها وأعرافها مَنفوشةٌ مثل سِربٍ من الطواويس. وخلفها قطيعٌ من الأفيال ترتدي قميصَ حمار الوحش وأنياباً من الأبنوس، وزرافاتٌ سُودٌ تحاول أن تمدّ أعناقها الى أغصان أشجار البَابَاي المُورِقة المُعلّقة في الفضاء. تتسابق سابحةً في الفضاء تماسيح بأحجامٍ ديناصورات. رذاذٌ لطيفٌ مُعطّرٌ برائحةٍ لم يَشمّها من قَبل يَتدفّق، وما إن تلمس خّبَائُه الأرضَ حتى تتشظّى وتَنبُت النوافير المُعطّرة، تتطاير منها فقاقيعُ شفّافةٌ، بداخلها أطفالٌ سُمْرٌ بملامحَ كيوبيديّة، طيوفُ أرواحٍ قُبّلَة تحاول أن تَثقبَها كي تتقمّصهم، لكن الفقاقيع الشّقيّة تبتكر لعبة التقافُز الطائر، وتنجو من فخاخها، وتتصاعَد إلى أعلى وتتركها حائرةً بعد أن وَصلت إلى مدىً لا تَتجاوزه، فتعود حسيرةً تقبع فوق حبيباتِ النَّدى العالقةِ بورودِ تايلانديّة.

تَفرقَعَت فجأةً ألعابٌ ناريّةٌ خَرج منها مُغنُّون بثيابٍ مكسيكيّة، صاروا مُعَلّقين في الفضاء قبل أن تطويهم سحابةٌ بيضاءُ عملاقةٌ بجوفها، حين توقّفت عصفورة الحياة عن تغريدها البهيج والتفتَت إليه مذعورةً وهي تُشير إلى السّحابة التي صارت على مَرمى ريشةٍ منها وتكاد أن تبتلعها، ثم إلى صديقه الغارق الذي انشغَلَ عنه بِبَعْثِ الألوان، فصار يَشهَقُ شَهقاتٍ مُتلاحقةً ويُباديه كي يُنقذَه من الغَرَق. حَدّق مَشدُوهاً في عينَي عصفورة الحياة، التي بدأ البياضُ في التهامِها ولم يَبْق منها غير رقبتها التي تُزَيّنُها حزوزٌ زرقاءُ وصفراءُ، فتَبَيّن له، عندما رأى دُعزَها يُطِلّ من عينيها، أنّهما عينا مَن طَرّعَ أنّها أخلفَت موعدَها معه قبل صعوده الأخير. التفتَت صوب صديقِه الصغير عازماً على أن يُدركه هذه المرّة، فوَجد النهر قد تحوّل إلى أكوامٍ مُمتدّةٍ من الكُثبانِ البَيضَاء.

بيرث، ١٩ أبريل ٢٠١٠م

*عفيف إسماعيل، كتاب مثلما ينام الضوء بعيداً، دار النسيم للنشر والتوزيع، القاهرة ٢٠١٣م

The Girls Home

MYKAELA SAUNDERS

Jadie wakes up, breathless and sweaty beneath the scratchy blanket. She panics. Where is she?

The dark room breathes in and out with dozens of snores from all directions.

It's too dark to see anything, but in the bed next to Jadie's someone tosses and turns and mumbles in a familiar way. Jadie listens: it sounds like — yes, it is — her cousin Krystal. That girl has an unmistakably squeaky voice.

Jadie is relieved, but then she remembers where they are.

Deep inside this decrepit old factory where they are locked up, where they all live and work together, Jadie inhales the smell of her fellow young women — of sleeping breath spiked with night sweats, and a cocktail of hormones mixed with fear and rage and longing, and secret buried dreams.

From the bed on Jadie's other side, a hand reaches out and pats her mattress. Jadie grabs Danny's hand and squeezes it.

'Bad dreams, my girl?' asks Jadie, very soft.

Danny whispers, 'Yeah. I was dreaming about my family again, but it didn't seem like they really were my family.'

'C'mon then.' Jadie lifts her blanket up and once Danny jumps in she closes it back over.

'I'm getting worried, Jades,' Danny says, facing her. 'I can't remember much about my family anymore.'

'Same here, Dan. I'm forgetting them too. I can't remember what Mum's voice sounds like.'

'Me too. And all my family's faces are a blur. When I try and remember Mum's face, it swims around and fades. I can't hold her still in my mind.'

Jadie whispers, 'I can't even remember coming here.'

'Me neither. And I don't remember much about my life before here.'

Danny rolls over. Jadie wraps her arm around her and says, 'I know that I knew you and some of the other girls from before. But everyone else is strange in here. Some of them don't even seem real.'

Danny nods. They hold their breath; footfalls echo along the hall outside their room. When the noise fades, Danny says, 'Maybe we suppressed our memories. I think I learnt something, before all this, about how our minds block things out so we can just get on with things.'

'Do you reckon they did something to us Dan?'

'Who knows with these dogs. I wouldn't put anything past them.'

Footfalls again. The girls wait.

'It's like, the more time that goes on, the more we forget who we were before,' says Danny.

'Do you reckon they're putting something in our food or water? To make us forget, to keep us in line?' asks Jadie.

'Wouldn't surprise me. My gran used to tell me that they'd dope the girls up in the home she was in.'

'That's fucked.' Jadie breathes out. 'I don't even know how long we've been in here. Do you?'

'No idea, tid. It feels like I've always been here, but I do remember some bits from before. Like, I remember when I was little. And I remember my family's stories of places like this too.'

'This place reminds me of the places Nan and Gran used to be in. I remember them telling me those yarns. It's weird, don't ya reckon?'

'True. And it seems like nothing's really changed since those days,' says Danny.

The girls wait out another round of footfalls. Jadie says, 'We need to get the fuck outta here Dan.'

Danny nods her head. 'We will, I swear to god.'

The high up windows begin to brighten, bringing pale light into the room. The girls stop talking and let their minds wander, knowing they haven't got long to go before there'll be no more time for daydreaming. No room for joy or rest in this place.

Danny pats Jadie's leg. 'I better hop back over now.'

'Righto sis.' Jadie squeezes Danny's shoulder and she gets back into her own bed. Both girls pull their blankets back over them.

Soon: the familiar click, buzzing wires, and bright lights flare on overhead.

'Morning workers!' A deep voice booms into the room. 'Up and ready in ten minutes!'

The guard flicks the lights on and off. With his other arm, he holds his gun like a lover.

Along the room's two long walls, girls jump out of beds, moving like stop-motion figures in the flickering. They are bleary with sleep, and their shorn hair sticks up this way and that.

The only one still in bed is Natty-girl, who stays under the covers with her eyes squeezed shut to avoid an episode; when she hears the guard has stopped flicking, she rolls out of bed too. The guard leaves the room.

As Jadie yawns and stretches, she gives her middle finger to the camera on the ceiling. She knows it's only there for show because she's never been disciplined for her morning ritual.

The girls undress from their nightwear into stiff beige cotton dresses. Impractical clothes for practical work. Skinny legs of all shades of skin poke out beneath the knee-length hems, as arms set to tying shoes and making their beds, ready for another day of mind-numbing, back-breaking work, in this dull world of hospital green and grey.

The girls pour out of the room to the bathrooms to ready themselves for work.

In the dining hall later that morning, the girls eat their breakfast at long tables. Jadie sits with her friends — except for Joanne, who is at the kitchen serving the porridge she made for everyone.

'How'd youse all sleep?' Jadie asks.

'Like shit,' says Krystal. 'Nightmares again.'

'Us too,' say Jadie and Danny, fingers pointing to themselves, then each other.

'Aw, you poor things,' says Natty-girl.

'Ancestors are warning us of something,' says Lani.

'Can't for the life of me think of what they'd be tryna warn us about,' says Tahnee. 'Nothing off about our situation at all.'

They all giggle — quietly.

Krystal says, 'I dreamt Mum was sick. Dreamt she was real skinny and crook from not eating. I woke up crying through the night.'

'Aw bub, that's no good. That's just this place getting to you, making your brain play tricks on you. Doesn't mean she's really sick,' says Danny.

'Yeah, but how would I even know either way? I haven't spoken to her for years. So, she could be sick for all I know.'

Natty-girl scrapes the last of the creamy oats out of her bowl, and says, 'Well, I dreamt that I knew where we are. I figured it out from where the sun rises and sets, and by the smells outside, and the noises from over the fences. But I can't remember now.'

Everyone's faces rise then fall.

'Well, maybe this means you will figure it, hey girl?' says Jadie. Natty-girl shrugs.

Lani taps the table. 'Hey, we get our new job rosters today!'

'Thank fuck. I am sick of working inside. I'm starting to turn gub.' Krystal flexes her fair-skinned hand.

'Look out! You couldn't be gub if you fucken tried,' says Tahnee, pulling a woolly ringlet. 'Look at this wild hair!'

The girls take their empty bowls up to the kitchen; Krystal hangs behind and nudges Jadie, and asks quietly, 'Why you gotta egg Natty-girl on for? You know she's not all there.'

'I'm not egging her on. And don't be mean.' Jadie nudges her back. 'She is all there, she's just a bit different to us.'

'I just don't think you should get her hopes up too much.'

'If anyone's gonna figure it out it'll be her. We're not as smart as her.'

Krystal cocks an eyebrow.

'I'm serious,' says Jadie. 'Why do you think she's so good at drawing? She sees the world differently. And none of us are close to figuring it out.'

A guard calls out, 'Job lotto!'

The girls scurry back to their tables. The head guard unfolds a piece of paper and announces their new roles.

Each girl tenses or relaxes in turn, according to their new jobs.

The only one who keeps their old job is Krystal, who is assigned to the laundry again. She slams a hand on the table.

A young guard walks over and puts his hand on Krystal's shoulder. She shakes him off, stands up, and screams into his face, 'You promised!'

The guard backs away, hands up. More guards close in on Krystal, and drag her away as she cries, accusing the guard. He stands watching, clenching his jaw. He denies everything, and calls her a crazy girl.

When Krystal gets out of solitary a week later, she is just as furious as when the girls had last seen her. And whenever the guard is nearby, she hisses and mutters under her breath until her face turns purple.

'Sissy,' Jadie says to her one day. 'You're gonna have to cut this out or they'll throw ya back in there.'

'I'm trying, sis.' Krystal throws her hands up. 'But that lying cunt got my hopes up, then he dogged me.'

'What do you mean, tid?'

'We had a fucken deal.' She throws the laundry down and looks away. 'I sweet him up, and he gets me a job outside.'

Jadie blinks but she doesn't miss a beat. 'Well, maybe it's in his best interests to keep you in here.'

'Meaning what?'

'Well, if you was outside all day doing hard labour in the

sun, you'd be too tired and too ragged for him at the end of the day.'

'Hmmm,' Krystal says as she stands up a little straighter. 'True. And I wouldn't be as attractive to him all sweaty and sunburnt.'

'He probably just wants you in here closer to him.'

Krystal purses her lips. 'Truth is, he probably has no say in the roster, and just said he did to try and impress me. And I suppose I fell for it to make this all seem a bit more bearable.' She looks Jadie in the eye. 'Do you think less of me?'

'No way, my sister!' Jadie puts an arm around her. 'We all gotta do what we gotta do.'

'Well, in that spirit, I'm gonna use that motherfucker to get us all out of this place.'

The next day, Krystal and her guard are back to normal — her all sweet again, and him sneaking her extra food to share with her friends.

Over the coming weeks, Krystal asks him things here and there — about his life, about the weather, about the world outside. He's a little reserved but he does like showing off sometimes.

Krystal feeds the information to the other girls. Natty-girl uses scraps of paper to sketch out possible maps of the place. The maps change slightly each day, based on any new updates.

One morning Natty-girl announces: 'I think I've figured out the factory's layout, and where we are.' Lani looks around to make sure nobody is listening, and gestures for her to go on.

'I'm pretty sure we're in a warehouse in the industrial area of Ourimbah Road.'

The girls look around at each other, wide-eyed, excited.

'Not far from my old home,' says Jadie, eyes roving back and forth in the space over everyone's heads. 'If we can get out of here and get to mine, my family will help us out.'

'Well, I've hidden my maps at the back of the lowest laundry shelf if you want to see.'

Over the coming days, on each laundry shift, the girls take the maps out and study them, each adding their own notes with thoughts and sketches, and they start to make escape plans, based on their maps and new snippets of conversations. After each stealthy browse, the girls hide their precious notes away again under fluffy white towels.

The next week the girls are all on the same page. Over breakfast each day, they hash out their escape plans, testing weak spots through questioning until there are none left.

On the scheduled evening, Krystal leads her guard into their special abandoned storeroom. Joanne watches from the stall where she's been hiding. She gives them a few minutes then sneaks up behind him. He is too distracted to notice Joanne cover his face with a cloth soaked in kitchen-cleaning chemical. He fights for a few seconds and goes limp; the girls try not to breathe it in.

The girls take his gun and strip him of his uniform, tie him up to the metal shelves and tape his mouth up. Joanne, the girl with the most similar to build to him, rolls a tight bandage around her torso to strap her big chest down and puts his uniform on, boots, hat and all. The girls use his keys to lock the storeroom behind them.

Hat down low over her eyes, Joanne leads her fake lover down the long corridor.

'You're carrying the gun upside down,' Krystal whispers, 'Spin it 'round. And walk heavier.'

And Joanne does, walking with less of a swing in her hip, and more of a thrust, her boots a steady beat over the green lino floor.

None of the other guards even look at them. They've always turned a blind eye; what they don't see, they can't get in trouble for not reporting.

Joanne walks Krystal out of the building, and then she hides her inside the jeep parked in the shadows near the fence.

They wait: Krystal covered with blankets in the back of the jeep, and Joanne leaning against the fence, so that if anyone comes out they will think the guard is pissing.

Over in the dinner hall, the other girls eat together, each deep in their own thoughts.

Jadie only pretends to eat; something feels off to her. There aren't as many guards on the dinner shift as usual, which means they'll be out prowling and more likely to catch the girls when they do their runner.

Jadie starts to agonise. She doesn't want anyone to get caught but she doesn't want to leave anyone behind either. She knows they'll have more success if only a handful of them escape — those known and trusted to each other — rather than trying to get everyone out at once.

They can always come back for the ones left behind once they've raised the alarm in the outside world — but nobody will even make it that far if they aren't all smart about it.

And if those left behind can see that this can be done, well, that is just as good as handing them a key as far as Jadie is concerned.

Jadie stands up. She signs to Natty-girl and Danny and Lani and Tahnee to stay put and trust her, and walks over to the other side of the room where most of the guards are. She picks a girl at random and pulls her off her seat. Jadie shapes up to the girl and shoots out a quick jab into her surprised face. She clocks her on the jaw — but not too hard. She wants a fight, not a knock-out.

The girl is wild. She shakes the sting off and flies at Jadie with an elbow, catching her on the temple. Every girl has crowded around now and is cheering them on.

The guards swarm in too.

Jadie's friends sneak out the other door unnoticed. They keep down low and run like buggery down the corridor.

When they get to the door Danny knocks: one-two, one-two, one, before they open it.

Joanne hears the knock and meets them at the door. She leads Natty-girl and Danny and Lani and Tahnee to the jeep. Her quizzical eyebrows are answered with shaken heads. They pile on top of Krystal, and they all squash themselves down in the back and cover themselves with dark blankets.

It is a hot and dusty ride, but once Joanne yells out that they are safely outside of the perimeters of the compound, they fling the blankets off and peek out the windows at the outside world, laughing and hugging each other.

Meanwhile, back in the dinner hall, Jadie puts on a show as the guards drag her away from the other girl. They are both bloody and bruised and panting.

Jadie screams out to the watching girls about how much worse it will get for them if they all stay complicit. None of the girls look like they trust her much after this incident, but she can see that some of them believe what she is saying. She concentrates on them.

Jadie urges them: 'You're all somebody, back in your old lives. Don't ever forget that! Because if you forget, this will turn into hell for all of you, and all because of what they want you to do. Everyone of you will be betrayed and controlled by each other, and every one of you will have to betray to have any control.'

Most of the girls look away as the guards march Jadie past them.

Jadie tries for one last rallying cry: 'These guards need you! They need your bodies and your labour, so deny them everything! Go on strike, never give them an inch, and consent to nothing! Stand up to them always. They need you subservient to exploit you!'

Jadie is dragged kicking and screaming to the medical bay, where she is heaved onto a bed and strapped down.

A nurse sticks a needle into her arm.

I hope the girls got out safe, is her last thought before she passes out.

*

Jadie wakes up in a room that's so bright she scrunches her eyes shut again immediately. She slowly adjusts to the light by peeking through her eyelashes. She can't shield her eyes with her hands because she's strapped down to a padded chair. She's held there by a thick metal strap across her chest and upper arms, another across her hips, and smaller straps over her wrists and ankles.

There is some part of her panicking, somewhere deep down, but it is shrouded in a heavy blanket of peace and calm. A drip feeds liquid into her arm. Surrounding Jadie's chair, data lit up on holographic screens showcases her heart rate, blood pressure and other vital signs.

'Where am I?' she asks, tongue thick and sleepy.

'Good afternoon, Jadie.' A chirpy voice diffuses through the room. 'You are in the VR room of Initi-corp. You have just finished playing the Girls Home simulation from the Emerging Elders program, and you are being sedated while you readjust to reality.'

Jadie chases slow thoughts around her mushy brain. She catches one.

'Those last few years in that place was all just a game?' The words come wet from her drenched mouth. She slurps at the saliva dripping from her lip.

'No, not a game. It was a simulation, and you were only in there for half an hour.'

With what little strength she can summon, Jadie throws her head back and screeches through her teeth. Her hands clench into fists and she bucks her body against the chair.

She feels her vein grow cold as the voice says, 'We'll let you sleep a little more now, and when you wake up we'll have a debrief session. We will answer all of your questions then.'

The next time Jadie wakes up she's been moved to another room and all the other girls are there. They are all still strapped to their chairs, and have been arranged around a round table; where their drips had been, each girl now has a bright flouro bandaid on their inner elbow. The girls smile at each other with relief. They are a little groggy, but much more lucid than on their first awakening.

A holographic face appears in the centre of the table — but the face that looks out at each girl is different. Jadie sees her Nan, Danny sees her Uncle, and the others see their most beloved Elders too. These faces speak with one voice.

'It's good to see you all relaxed and smiling again. It takes a little while to adjust back, and we've found that having you all debrief together takes some of the sting out of this for you.'

'Why would youse do this to us though?' asks Danny.

'You all begged for this!'

The girls gasped in unison.

'You were all selected from a highly competitive process for our cultural program for community leadership training. There are a few different kinds of initiations; this one was designed to see how community-minded you are. We wanted to see whether you would roll over and cop it, or if you would tell your keepers where to go. Those of you who rebel, who look out for others, who keep culture alive, have got a good chance of becoming good community leaders.'

'Pretty convoluted way of going about it if you ask me,' says Krystal.

'The point is to see whether you would pass these tests. And that's important to us as a community: it shows us that we grew you up properly, that we told you the proper stories, and gave you the right skills and knowledge you need to resist these situations.'

Jadie scowls; her sedative has almost worn off. 'I don't see how you can make this test all about you when we were the ones who took it.'

'It's like a school test, see? If some students fail and some pass, that doesn't say much. But if lots of students fail or if lots of students pass, then that's on the teacher either way.'

Tahnee says, 'I still don't see the point of it.'

'You young ones are at risk of losing culture. You're always on your phones these days, and carrying on about how hard you've got it when the truth is that you have it made. So, we designed this sim to see how you stack up.'

'Well, you older ones might know culture but this is straight-out child abuse,' says Joanne.

Krystal nods. 'Whatever your reasons, I can't imagine why anyone would put young girls through something so cruel,' she says.

'You didn't actually go through anything. But your old people, they really *did* go through all that, unlike you lot. You were only in there for half an hour, and now you're all making out like you've been victims of oppression!'

'It was hard in there, and you know it. Otherwise you wouldn't be trying to justify it,' says Danny. The other girls nod.

'Look,' say the faces. 'This is by far the worst thing any of you will have to go through in your lives. You mob have got it good. There is nothing hard about the way you live. We've eradicated poverty and inequality, there are no more wars, and no oppression, nothing. We live under our own law again. You younger generation have got it made, and all thanks to the hard work of your old people. If this was your greatest test in life, just be thankful it was only in your head.'

The girls, softened up now, all bow their heads.

'Still though,' says Lani. 'I don't understand why you had to traumatise us the way our old people were traumatised — just to see if we could handle it? Surely this can't be good for us.'

'You'll all be fine. Trust me. You were only in there for half an hour so you haven't missed out on anything. And there'll be no lasting damage as long as you talk it all out, and we have experts on hand to help you with that. Trauma only becomes post-traumatic if it isn't processed in the first few weeks or so. And none of you have work or study for the next two months. You all get an extended holiday to recuperate and process this before your mentorship officially starts.'

'I can't remember agreeing to this,' says Natty-girl.

'Me either,' the other girls say, and 'I didn't consent.'

'All of you girls consented to this. You all jumped at the chance because you know that it's a real privilege. Everyone knows what an honour it is to be able to say that you graduated from our program.' The voice chuckles through the room. 'You'll remember more and more over the coming days, once the drugs have worn off and you yarn to each other about it. It'll all come back to you.'

'Still, I can't really see me giving this the okay,' said Tahnee, and all the girls agree.

Krystal asks: 'And how do we know you're not making this up?'

'You all recorded your consent on film for this very reason.'

Six headsets drop down from the ceiling and clip over each girl's ears. 'You recorded these because you understood how hard it would be for you to believe at first. You can make up your minds after this.'

The hologram in the centre of the table morphs into a six-sided screen. Each girl sees a different screen, a paused clip that begins as a freeze-frame of themselves looking into the camera.

Through their headsets, the meta-Elder's voiceover says, 'We are recording these videos because when you come out of the simulation you will find it hard to believe anything we say. You are each recording a message to tell your future selves that you give free, prior and informed consent to this, with full support of your Elders as they appear in your personalised hologram. Please record a personalised message, and consider including something private so that your future self will believe this to be an authentic recording.'

On the screens, each girl unfreezes and speaks to their future selves.

Jadie watches herself on the screen, her eyes flicking back and forth as she reads from a prompt. 'I give free, prior and informed consent to this, and Nan approves too.' Now she looks directly into the camera. 'Jadie, you'll probably feel pretty wild about this, but I do really want to do it. It sounds like mad fun!' Then she leans forward. 'Oh, and just remember why you want to do this: you want to be a big part of the community like Nan is. And this'll help you get there. That's why we did this.'

And around the table, each girl relaxes as they listen to their past selves speaking messages of assurance to them in the here and now, suspicious and untrusting. The girls are quiet when the recordings finish and the screens turn back into their Elders' faces.

'How do we know you didn't fake these too?' asks Natty-girl.

'Yeah! This is exactly what I'd do to gain our trust,' says Krystal.

'Ah, but you already know deep down that it's true, don't you?'

The girls all look around at each other and nod.

'Anyways,' say the faces, 'the point is that you all passed your initiation with flying colours.'

The girls beam around at each other.

'Because,' the voice continues, 'the best community leaders are those who can put their own egos aside and reach across their differences to other people, even if there's nothing in it for them. People who do what needs doing to get the job done.'

The face turns into a six-sided screen again, and plays the same clip for each girl.

'Like Krystal,' says the voiceover, as a montage of Krystal's time in the home plays out. 'She put her own body on the line to get you out safely.'

The clip changes to a montage of Jadie.

'Jadie sacrificed herself too, to make sure the others got out safely. And people like Natty-girl here, who used her creativity and her intellect to figure out where you were being held. But also important are those who work quietly in the background — people who can look after everyone's basic needs, like Joanne here with her food and her resourcefulness. And those who always support others emotionally, even when they're the ones who need a shoulder to lean on, the way Danny does. People like Tahnee are important to keep peoples spirits up, and last but not least, there are those like Lani who won't let you forget your cultural ways.'

As each girl's highlight reel plays out they blush and smile.

The screens turn into faces again. 'See, the best leaders are those who bring out the best in people, not those who boss everyone around. You were all kind, creative and brave, you all looked out for your sisters, and you were all very, very clever. You kept your culture strong. You're all gonna make very good Elders one day.'

The metal straps holding each girl down open up and

slide back inside the chairs. The girls rub their wrists and flex their bodies.

'Now, you can all go eat, and start to process everything with your mentors. Then you can go catch up with each other properly. This will be the measure of your days for the next week or so, until your memories are restored.'

As the girls file out of the room, the faces add: 'And if you have any suggestions for improvement, please feel free to let us know. We'd love to improve the experience for the next cohort.'

And when the girls leave the next week, they stay away from their screens and games for a little while afterwards. They prefer to spend their time at the beach with each other, with the sun on their skin, blue sky above them and no walls or ceilings to keep them in.

Today, We Will Rise

MELEIKA GESA-FATAFEHI

The boy without a body watched as the sky caved in. No
one knew why. Well, no one important, according to the
men in white. He watched bewildered, and knew he could
do nothing, as pieces of the sky fell onto the mismatched
buildings people called home, where people worked, where
people died, trying to keep the facade going. This was a
quicker death. A death that was waiting for them, the boy
just didn't know death would be coming today.

Through the ash and the screams, seasick green and murky
purple smog from the not so dark night sky rushed into
the collapsing dome. Those who survived the debris would
not survive the air. They either died instantly or slowly,
choking on the poisons they were not used to. Their lungs
had never had to adapt to the outside world like those who
were from it. The boy without a body knew it was dusk,
that the real sun was going down, but the people inside had
been convinced it was day time. That the sun was always out

for eighteen hours. The boy without a body watched as the dome collapsed. The dome built by the rich colonisers to keep the poor outside, left to deal with the consequences of what the colonisers had done to his land — his country. In that moment, for the first time in a long time, since the first sunrise, the boy without a body felt like he could breathe.

Then he realised he was actually breathing.

*

I got in first. My heart was racing when I rushed through the doors as this world was ending. Ipi and Kyrie were outside using majik and our Skele-tons to control the laser beams the men in white used. Kyrie was connecting to the men in white's laser guns and twisting them into themselves, exploding them instantly. Ipi used majik instead, and tapped into the smog, using it as an extension of their body: where they moved, the smog moved. All they had to do was ask the smog to form shapes, this time it was whalebone spears and the smog listened, letting them fly straight into the hearts of the men in white.

The men in white never used their laser guns on their own kind, it was always on stun mode for them. But us, they'd aim for our heads or hearts even if we just spoke too loud. They'd tried to keep us all out, and for some time they did, but they also realised to survive the outside, they'd have to work with us, too. So they'd steal some of our children, or those old enough to work, and they'd live in the dome. I lived outside, on base, with the other villagers, but we snuck in sometimes to blend in, to make change and to one day, end it all.

I ran down the hallway, taking each turn like I remembered. Stairs, room 208, back door, down stairs, dark tunnel and then the last red door. I'd seen Ngarie do it a thousand times in the simulations. She taught me everything, even the steps to take to hack the main tiles on the dome, just in case she didn't come back. It was something she'd always say to prep for, to be ready for. I'd always tell her not to think like that, that she would always be here. But I should have listened to her then, I should have prepared myself, because one day she never did. I remembered it vividly, the night we decided to burn it all down. The night we failed. We didn't even reach the walls before we were surrounded by new recruits of the men in white. They wore baby blue coats, to mark their virginity in never taking a life and shield helmets that didn't allow you to see their faces. But I always knew there was a smile behind it all; they loved killing us. It was a type of sport for them.

Before I could react and even think about the type of majik I wanted to use, Ngarie sucked her teeth and turned to me.

Her eyes said it all, but she said it aloud too. 'Sorry' was all she said as she reached for my face, brushing my cheek. She smiled briefly, as if for reassurance, as if this were how I would want to remember her. Her red Afro out reaching for the holographic sky, her face marked in our tribal colours, red and white lines down her nose which looked like mine, surrounded by killers. I could feel my body stretch and shrink in one instance, and just like that, I was somewhere else. She'd done a transport spell, which hadn't been done in a long time without severely injuring the spellcaster. She knew this; she'd rather go out by her own hands than theirs. I heard the orders from my new location, 'Don't kill the feral. Supreme wants to talk to this one.'

I turned around and realised she'd transported me onto the rooftop of a nearby building. I fell to the floor immediately. Using my Skele-ton I asked her to talk to me, say anything to me, but she never replied. She knew if she did, that I would talk her out of it, like I always do. She would always say that I was the brains, and she was the muscle. She would train everyday just so she could become stronger, not because it made her a good fighter, but because the stronger you were, the stronger your magic. In this moment, it was the very first time I had ever seen her weak. She was on her knees hunched over, holding her chest. She looked at them, blood running down her nose, and carefully stood up, making sure no matter how much her body swayed, she was upright.

She spat blood out before wiping the blood off her nose, smearing and mixing our tribal colour with her blood. She looked at her hands, and a smile spread across her face, a laughter gurgled out, it wasn't like anything she'd ever shared before. It sounded menacing, purposeful, as if she knew something they didn't. It was at that moment I knew what she was going to do. Use blood majik.

She looked at each of them before mustering up the strength to spit out 'You think you've won. But you will lose. We will RISE and your blue and white coats—' she coughed into her hands and looked down to see more blood. Her smile grew wider, and she laughed louder, uncontrollably now, as she said it '… will be covered in red.'

With that, the blood on her hands and face separated themselves from her skin and formed little spheres and with one twist of her wrist, shot through the air going straight through the coats of the men in front of her. Piercing their armour and helmets. Before the others behind the frontline could do anything, she reached behind her ear and placed the small pill all RISE fighters get, swallowed and just like that her body dropped to the floor, lifeless.

I saw the men in white take turns in slicing a piece of her off. They took her deep brown eyes, the same as our mother's, who established the resistance: RISE. I was always jealous mine weren't the same shade, but I was glad she did have her eyes, because it felt like my mother was never really gone; I'd just look at Ngarie and see her face. It took them a couple of slicing, but they had taken her ears too, the same ears we'd pierced with whale bone to mark her passage into adulthood. She'd squirmed when Ipi slit it open, and she had held onto my hand tighter, but never made a sound; she was always trying to be strong like that. It felt like she'd crushed the bones in my hands, but I let her. I'd do anything for my older sister. The last thing they took were her index fingers and thumbs, the same fingers she used to lock the hacking channel RISE used within the dome and outside of it. After a little chuckle from the some of the men in white soldiers handing their trophies to their fellow rookies who snickered in disgust, the lead officer, the only one in white, reached into his coat for the elixir they use to disintegrate bodies. He opened the small vial and with a pipette dropped a single drop of the essence onto her body and before I could register the death of the last family member I had, Ngarie melted into blood and bones. They left her there for the road side cleaners to wipe her clean off this earth. They took her Skeleton and never turned back, picking up the bodies of their dead as they went, one by one, still talking about their new trophies from the latest wilding.

I don't remember much after that, all I can recollect is running through the city, hiding in the shadows from the men in white, who were circling the area looking for the second suspect who disappeared in front of their eyes. I remember running through the sewers, then the tunnels, stomach turning, from all the smells, and daylight dancing at the exit, waiting for me, wanting to embrace me, I remember throwing up everything I had eaten in a week as soon as I reached base. I couldn't even cry at first, I just sat and stared at any inanimate object, wondering what would have happened if I had done something different. If I had just insisted we stayed home, stay on base and go another day. But I hadn't and it ate away at my edges. My own comrades and best friends — Ipi, Kyrie and Flora — couldn't even pull me out of it. I think I didn't want to be saved. So they did what they could do: feed me, watch me and stay with me, till I was ready.

It was Flora who brought me back from drowning in my thoughts. She had sat next to me as I sat underneath the stars, staring at the new statue of Ngarie right next to our mother's. She had led the RISE, just like my grandmother, just like my sister. The statues were made of clay and stood between the only underground entrance that led into the dome from the outside. There were many clay statues, one made for every life lost to the dome, for every body incinerated inside and never given the right to return to their ancestors the way they wanted. Flora had sat in silence, watching the stars with me. Before the sun could rise, she reached for my hand and squeezed, whispering, 'I miss her laugh the most, you know. It always echoed, always filled a place up.'

She smiled at me and I realised that I had forgotten I wasn't the only one grieving. So was Flora, Ngarie's girlfriend. So were my friends, my village, my countrymen. I held onto her hand tighter and did the one thing I couldn't do before: cry.

It took weeks for me to recover from injuries sustained in the transport spell and train through simulations to get everything right. We had nothing on the outside, no tech, which is why RISE always pirated and hacked. The outside was getting better because of it. We built air purifiers for families whose blood was taking longer to adapt to the air. We built food modifiers to make sure whatever grew in the poisoned soil was still edible; but we could never figure out how to make the food delicious. We built projecting simulators to recreate stories about our creation stories and how the dome was built, but also to train those old enough to fight. RISE built tech that wasn't available inside the dome either, like the tech skeletons we called Skele-tons. It was tech combined with majik. It allowed people who belonged to the land to interact with tech but also with those who had a Skele-ton attached to their body. Skele-tons were alive, an extension of our minds, our upper hand against the men in white and their supreme.

It was the very same Skele-ton I had to place in the eighth chamber behind the red door, in the supreme's building, the headquarters of the men in white. Their supreme, Michelle Johnson, was the seventh Michelle who'd been appointed supreme, coming into leadership when his father had died of old age. Dying from old age is a privilege not afforded to those outside the dome. Seven generations of white men who only cared for their own and for those who didn't care for those who were from the very land they poisoned. Seven generations of torture. Seven generations of deaths. Within seven generations my father's Island had sunk and he led his people here, to my mother's country. He had died while mum was pregnant with me and Ngarie. Ngarie was born first. She'd always exclaim it was because she wanted to check if the world was safe for me. She said it wasn't, which is why she decided to always protect me; she never knew I decided the same. Dead was one of the first clay statues built. Mum said I looked like him, shaggy curls, deep ochre eyes like honey, full lips and a gap between our two front teeth. She said that our skin looked like the night sky had wrapped us both with a piece of her and gave us two stars for eyes.

I had taken out the ceiling of the dome, but to dismantle the walls we'd have to hack directly from the supreme's headquarters. Which is why I was here, underground searching, looking for the eighth chamber. I used my hands and dug behind the wires of the walls, searching for the carving of number eight. I couldn't find it on the wall on the left so I continued to the next, my hands searching and feeling for the numbers. I felt six and seven, and before I knew it I had found the number eight carved. With that, I closed my eyes and focused on entering the main frame. The sensation of interacting with technology was always weird, like a buzzing feeling in your body that slithers in all directions. But connecting to something so big, so 'alive', had made me feel as if the floor beneath me was no longer there and that I was falling. The first thing I saw was entangled numbers, forming knots, and vines, I had to rip them apart, but every time I did, felt like I had burnt my hands. I had to concentrate, think for what I wanted, and the vines started to clear themselves, forming pathways. I searched folders, corners, spaces for a switch, for a code, for a sign to dismantle the walls but nothing. I knew I was running out of time; I knew the men in white would check on their tech quarters at any moment. Before I could give up and join Ipi and Kyrie, who were on the ground using their Skele-tons to control machinery against the men in white, I heard a familiar voice reach out for me.

'Iratakki? How'd you get in here?' Ngarie looked the same as she did, brown eyes, big red hair, and the scar on her chin that matched mine, from arrow practice when we were ten. She asked again, this time with fear, 'How'd you get in here, Ira? Only the dead can get in here.'

I looked at her, confused. 'What do you mean, Nganga. I'm in the mainframe, trying to shut it down.' She smiled and rushed into me, hugging me tightly and then holding my face. 'I transferred my entire mind to my Skele-ton.'

'What … how'd you do that?'

'It doesn't matter right now, what matters is that you know I'm still somewhat alive, and so is Mum and so are many others.'

'What do you mea—' But before I could say anything more, she took my hand and we zoomed through the pathways and entered a room with a red lever.

'This is the switch Ira. I figured out how they do it, how they run this place.'

'How?' I exclaimed so confused, so worried.

'The elixir: it traps our souls. They use our souls as energy to run this place. It's why we can communicate with the tech so easily — it's made of us.'

She pulled me toward the lever and placed my hand on it. 'As soon as you push this down, not only will those walls fall, but all the souls they've been using … we'll be setting them free, but some of them will return—'

'Return?'

'They didn't just trap souls, Ira. This place is also powered by our gods.'

I looked at her and knew what she meant. If our gods can return, so can the dead. She held my face again. 'When you push it down, come find me and Mum. The boy will tell you everything.' And before I could ask for clarification, she had disappeared. I paused and looked at the lever. My people died for this moment. For this to all end, and I was here, instead of my sister, mother, grandmother ... I said the only thing I could say before pushing it down: 'We will rise again.'

*

The boy without a body watched as people who had similar faces to those he once called family, used majik and tech against the very people who destroyed his country. He watched as purple-green spears flew into the bodies of those as white as the linen they wore on Sundays. He watched as they fell on the ground, as hands springing from the earth claimed their souls. Those who weren't like him couldn't see those hands or hear the words that were being chanted from underneath the soil; remember us, remember us, remember us ...

The boy without a body knew the dead were going to rise again. He could feel a faint heartbeat where a heart should be in his chest. He knew something was changing. The walls of the dome were disintegrating. Unlike the ceiling of the dome made of tech, the walls were made of simulation tiles. He knew he was no longer confined to this dome. He could finally visit his birth place and speak to his sister in the bottom of the river. But before he could leave, he felt a hand on his shoulder and spun around to the familiar faces looking directly into his eyes. 'Hey, we're getting out of here, our people are outside, would you like to join us?'

With that, the boy without a body, was just a boy and he knew, there was work to be done.

Mami Wata

SISONKE MSIMANG

If you marry mami water
Make you dey ready to waka
Fit to carry you enter water
Oh you no go come back again

Yemi Alade

Mami Wata lay on the beach cradling a dead woman's child. The mermaid was the last of her kind; the only seawoman left. The dead child on the other hand, was the first of many. He wore a yellow jacket and still clutched a small suitcase filled with his tiny belongings. In the weeks to follow, dead children would wash ashore by the thousands. Where they had once arrived on the red continent as refugees, now they landed as corpses. Each beloved child had been sent on a hopeless journey, seeking dry land and a place where the seas would not encroach.

The boy's mother had saved food for months, stitching miniscule sacs filled with morsels of dried fruit and meat into his clothing for the trip that would either save his life or end it. She told him not to share any of it unless he was certain there was enough to sustain him. Others would have to find their own ways of surviving, she told him. He nodded and asked where she would be. She had not known how to answer, and so rather than lie, she told him the truth. She said she would be praying for him from the shore, and because he was still too small to understand the meaning of the word abandonment, he smiled and said thank you and this broke her heart more than she had imagined was possible.

She put him on the boat wearing his favourite yellow jacket. She made sure he was in the middle of the crowded vessel and surrounded by other children. A teenager took his hand and both of them looked so very small — a girl and a boy about to capsize. And yet the massive continent on the other side of the waves was one of the only places left where children stood a chance of surviving the rising seas which had swallowed up all the places where the wealthy had once holidayed. Her own archipelago had disappeared in just five years — one island submerged at a time until there was nothing to do but leave.

She watched from the shore for a while, until the boat had tipped over onto the side of the world she could not see. She was breathless with anxiety, knowing that she would never see him again. Then she gathered her courage and walked alone to the other side of the island. She got into the water and swam past the break. She had always been an efficient swimmer and her instinct to stay afloat was strong. Still within hours she was under the sea, the current had dragged her under and this was a consolation.

The boy in the yellow jacket was the only one on the boat whose body made it to shore. The others disappeared into the ocean's depths — and perhaps washed up elsewhere. He had been spared this cold anonymity because Mami Wata had plucked him from the current and cradled him in her arms. She had swum gracefully and with great purpose, knowing that there is nothing more precious in this world than a motherless child.

After him there were more deaths. More brown children washed up on the shore. They began to arrive at an alarming rate; their small bodies tossed this way and that by the boiling sea. The boy in the yellow jacket was the first though. Mami Wata had sung him to the beach and then, seeing how badly ulcerated his skin had become from the chemicals in the water, she caressed him and rubbed his back. In Mami Wata's arms he was free of pain and the melody of the mermaid's song carried him to his mother's spirit.

*

There had once been an army of them, thousands of water deities, part woman, part fish. They were as plentiful as the ripples in a lagoon and as common as waves in the ocean. They were born to ease the pain of death for their two-legged sisters and brothers who died at sea. They lived on the coast as well. Sometimes they sat on the shore, plaiting one another's hair and resting in the sun. The sea goddesses were portals to the future. To those who needed memory, the mermaids offered a way to step back into the past. They took lovers who needed to forget and embraced those who wanted to remember.

Before there were thousands, there was only one.

*

Mami Wata had been born inside a lake, deep in a cave filled with the softest of currents and the sweetest of grasses. When she came up for air, for her very first breath, she had been awed by the wonder of life. She had slipped out of the water and looked at herself reflected in the lake, and she had been stunned by her own beauty. She had never set eyes on a single other soul and yet she knew that she was special.

She was Beyonce when the earth was still clay; so, so soft,

so jelly. She was Grace Jones in a suit of mirrors, so black, so lean, so sharp she could cut you, so sharp you dared not get too close — so sharp you had no choice. And yet she had no shape. Mami Wata moved like an octopus playing in technicolour. She was water, and the spirit of this — our first liquid — had been poured into Mami Wata the moment she had been conceived.

Mami Wata had been laid like an egg in the cave and she hatched in a lake which became the open sea. The shoreline above the lake was pristine and the forest that sloped gently away from the water on one side was home to the first animals that had ever walked. They roared and buzzed and were larger by far than the beasts and insects that had come after them.

One day Mami Wata felt the call of love. It began with a deep sense of curiosity — after all what is love if not curiosity for another? She decided to explore, to swim from the lake into the river in search of something new. She would swim — she thought to herself — until she felt she was no longer alone.

She emerged where the river's mouth met the ocean, finding herself in a lagoon. The birds looked down and were stunned by her fins and awed by the expanse of her hair which floated like its own separate entity, a silver cloud full of ripples, a mighty Afro that set off her shimmering blue-black skin.

She had chanced upon Nyami's bay, though of course there is a way of seeing her arrival not as luck but as providence. Nyami was the eldest son of the river, and also the most temperamental. He heard the commotion of the birds and went to see what was happening. He rode the strong current of the river, angry — as usual — because he did not appreciate the interruption. He had been pining for the rain, wondering when she might appear again, and hating himself for spending so much time fretting about her. She came when she came, and always, she greeted him in the same way — as though she had never left at all.

He had first fallen in love with the rain when they were children. She loved him too. She lavished him with attention. But over time he realised she was inconsistent. Sometimes she promised to come, and wouldn't. Then, when he was on the verge of giving up, she would arrive bearing gifts — flowers and berries and seeds and burbling laughter. Other times, just as he was preparing to go fishing, she would appear unannounced and angry, lashing him with her tears. He loved her in all her moods and incarnations. How could he not? He was the son of the river.

So Nyami emerged from the river and saw Mami Wata waist deep in the water. She looked like she was expecting him. She had felt his energy move through the water and so in a way she was not surprised. She knew she was enchanting, and understood the effect her beauty had on others. She knew this simply from looking at Nyami's face. She understood that his awe was not singular; that all who saw her would be similarly startled. She understood also that this was part of the fate of a deity. Beauty humbled and confused men, and yet it was such a silly thing — how one looked. Mami Wata understood the moment she saw Nyami that men were not to be taken too seriously. Over time this sense would be underscored for her, time and again. So many of them were unable to see beyond the surface, so many were fooled by appearances, mesmerised and distracted by matters of no substance. It would be women who would hold Mami Wata's attention and earn her respect. Men would be playthings to her, but it would be women who would be Mami Wata's greatest friends and most fearsome protectors. In the meantime, it would be Nyami who would help build her army.

Mami Wata smiled at the strong man who stood in the forest and then swam up close. She motioned for him to get in. He jumped in without hesitation. This only confirmed her instincts: not very bright.

They circled one another in the water. She flirted and he was flattered. His face glowed and he began to remember what it had been like when he first encountered the rain. Very quickly, he was telling her of his heart's desires. He even cried, telling her about his lost love.

'I hate her,' he exclaimed, and Mami Wata wiped his face and told him that he could no sooner hate rain than he could hate himself.

Mami Wata slowly explained that he was part of a delicate balance: without rain the waters of the river could never flow. His life force depended on the rain. You cannot hate the parts of the earth that allow you to exist.

They had climbed out of the water then, and Mami Wata had transformed into a two-legged woman. She had not known she possessed this power, that she only had to think it and it would be done. And so they sat on a large rock and held one another in silence, with only breath punctuating their longing. She told him — wordlessly — how to love the beauty he held within himself and they fell asleep on the rocks.

When they awoke in the morning, as the dawn pinked the forest, Nyami taught her the songs of the birds. She joined him, humming the tunes of the fish. Her voice was low and loose and his was high and delicate; together they were a symphony of water burbling.

Mami Wata and Nyami conceived and soon after their time together, Mami Wata left Nyami and returned to the lake. When her time came she laboured and laughed with the pain of childbirth and at the right hour the rain came and mother wind delivered a breeze and the mermaid laid so many eggs they spread across the lake like a curtain of foam.

When they hatched, Mami Wata had her army. They grew to be as large as the women warriors of Dahomey and as adept in the water as they were in the forests. Like their mother, they played in the lake getting stronger and fatter, preparing to be shown their destiny.

As they got sturdier, the mermaids roamed all the continent's waterways. They were playful and carefree mainly, though once in a while they came upon a lost soul; a mother overwhelmed by grief who had thrown herself into the river when it was at its fullest, or an accidental drowning. The mermaids swam these souls up, dragging their bodies to the riverbank or the lakeshore for their loved ones to find. They sang their names into the wind, and the trees became a chorus, announcing their deaths. This was why they were here; why they had been born and so they did not mind the sadness. As soon as a spirit had been accompanied they felt lighter. Often, they carried messages from the newly-dead to their loved ones. They would appear before a lover, or beckon a friend to the shore, and in this way the dead were always found, their bodies never lost.

As they grew into young women, Mami Wata allowed them to wander further away. One morning, as they bathed in the cool waters of the lake, one of the sisters heard a noise. It had come up through the springs that bubbled at the base of the lake. It was the saddest sound she had ever heard and it gripped her. She called the others and a few of them dove down, trying to find the sound. Others followed them and soon the river was clogged with mermaids, racing to the coast. They chased the sound of death; swimming towards a melancholy that could not be contained.

They moved as one, an army of goddesses swimming out to sea. They arrived in Nyami's lagoon just in time to see him snatched from the banks of the river. The slavers had arrived and mistaken him for a mortal man. It was only when he jumped in the water that he became like water, otherwise he looked like any other man.

He was forced onto the boat, joining many others. Strong and healthy young women and men who would never return. The mermaids followed the tall ship, an army of goddesses in hot pursuit of people-snatchers. They moved in a tight pack, a school of enraged women.

Suddenly they were no longer just daughters, they were queens — the Black queens of Atlantis, daughters of the under-waves who swam to resurrect the spirits of the dead and restore their dignity.

They followed Nyami to sea, not knowing that they would swim for four hundred years.

They never found him. Word was that he made his way to the slave blocks in Virginia and sired those slaves who grew wings and flew back. They heard this from the old Gullah women, the ones who spoke in a tongue the mermaids knew well — the language of their lake.

In his absence, they dove again and again and again into the ocean searching for the drowned and blessing the dead.

For four centuries Mami Wata and her children followed the ships from the west coast of their continent. The goddess army patrolled the seas, rescuing the dead and offering comfort to the living. They taught the slaves how to find joy again. They seduced men and caressed women and gave their lovers the pleasure they could not get on plantations and in the backrooms of kitchens. Their lovers in turn gave the warriors ways to remember them — mementos the mermaids would wear in their hair, mirrors they would dangle from their ears and cowries they fixed to their waists and their hips.

The mermaids kept the drums of the river alive. They taught their husbands to sing and they made their wives hum. They turned love into body worship; taught their lovers how to wind their waists and roar with pleasure. Mami Wata and her adherents conjured the dead by stamping their feet. They summoned ancestors by shaking the earth and eating dust. They sang of love so the slaves could remember that they had been from somewhere; that they had been loved long before they were hated and were loved still.

One day, long after they had given up hope of ever finding Nyami, Mami Wata saw a bird falling into the sea. It was him — the father of her daughters and the son of the river. She could see the lines of him in the set of the bird's beak and in the span of its wings. The bird hit the water hard and Mami Wata and her daughters gathered around to catch its fall with their tails. They lifted the animal high and it flapped its wings in fright and bewilderment, and then took off, climbing higher and higher; heading towards the East. It was Nyami for sure; they could hear the thunder in his wings. He had been water, then flesh and was now a bird, a spirit sailing through the sky, on its way to meet other waters.

*

In time the slave boats stopped. The sharks no longer circled the ships, and the mermaids were able to rest. The warriors stayed in the places where they were most beloved — in the waterways of Angola where Kianda was the high priestess, and at the southern-most tip of Africa where Mamobolo reigned. Mami Wata nestled in the creeks of Columbia where her followers called her Mohana, or Madre de agua and frolicked in the waves off the coast of Bahia where they called her Yimanja and praised her beauty by sacrificing a white chicken.

Shrines in her honour appeared on rocks along the shoreline, where she might pass. Church masses presided over by the descendants of slaves honoured her as the angel of the ocean and the mother of the seas.

*

A hundred years after the slave ships stopped, the icebergs began — imperceptibly — to melt. Around the same time, poison began to accumulate in the seas. Mami Wata remembered swimming off the coast of Brazil and tasting dead water for the first time. It was a distinct, metallic taste. The ocean there had a heaviness that did not belong in the seas. She had led her sisters into a cloud of runoff from the Amazon. It had been so foul that many of the warriors had been stunned by it. They had never encountered such a noxious smell before — the body parts of cattle bobbing in the sea mixed in with fertiliser and oil and the sewage of the hundreds of millions who lived off the generosity of the ailing river.

When Mohana, the first mermaid became ill, it began with lethargy and quickly progressed to fits. The same fate befell the others: mermaid after mermaid gagged on the poison in the seas and grew pale and thin.

Though mermaids were supposed to be immortal one morning they found Yimanja — the strongest of all Mami Wata's generals — floating on the water's surface. Her silver hair fanned out like mercury and her lips were a purple bruise.

After Yimanja's passing, the army was hit hard. They began to sink in large numbers, sometimes as many as thirty at a time. Some could not breathe — there were pieces of polystyrene in their windpipes. Others fell soundlessly to the seabed; their bodies made heavy by plastic baubles trapped in their gills. Mermaid corpses piled up on the bed of the Atlantic, taking their place alongside the bones of slaves.

*

Alone without her daughters, Mami Wata realised that the sea — for so long her place of respite — would eventually turn against her. She thought back to the clouds of poison that curled out from the Amazon and the Congo, and she understood, finally, that some innate quality in the element of water had shifted and it was no longer what the sea

carried that harmed the creatures in the ocean. It was the
ocean water itself that had been inalterably damaged.

*

Having lost her children, Mami Wata gathered her strength.
She decided to swim east in the direction Nyami had flown.
She had to tell him that the waters had turned toxic; that the
rain would be full of the same poisons and that his father the
river would soon be so sick he would dry out. She knew that
in the telling there would be release; that the burden of the
tragedy would be halved.

She had chanced upon the boy in the yellow jacket as
she raced towards Nyami. She had been touched by his
smallness, by his suitcase, by the freshness of his haircut.
And so — though she was tired — she carried him at her
breast.

Arriving on the shore, Mami Wata kissed the child and
carried him to a nearby grove of samphire. She dug a grave
and placed a garland of saltbush around his neck and a
crown of wattle on his head. A fine prince.

Then she turned and looked inland at the desert, and at
the shining buildings and metal cranes, at the holes in the
distance that spoke of bottomless greed and destruction. She

looked up to the sky. Gow gow. A slow-winged heron looked down at her. Gow gow. It was Nyami. The bird swooped around and waited, using the wind to steady itself in the sky. Gow gow. Mami Wata stood to her full height, her legs getting accustomed to the sand. The bird blinked and turned and Mami Wata followed.

She understood. Nyami would take her to the spirits of this place but he understood that his powers — and hers — were of limited range here. Nyami could roam the sky but he could not mate. Though the skies were generous, this was not his country.

Still, Mami Wata was running out of time. She needed to speak to those who guarded the water; those who had the power to keep the water spirit pure and safe from the toxins of the sea. Sensing her impatience, the great bird swooped down and spoke to her. 'Slow down,' he said. 'The keepers of the source have lived with time for as long as time has existed and they have never tried to be its master. They have no respect for those who are in a hurry. They are not the pale men, the ones who believe they can make nature their servant. The keepers of the source will wait for you, and once we find them, they will listen.'

By nightfall Mami Wata could smell fresh water. She stopped and allowed herself to be tired. Nyami landed in a tree and watched as Mami Wata lit a fire to warm herself and to announce her presence. Within minutes another fire appeared and soon its holders had approached. The keepers had come to greet her.

They were her mother and her daughters, all the sea women who had ever lived stood in this place in the desert holding shields that were taller than men. They wore shells on their feet and at their waists and they were bare breasted and the colour of dust and mud and the desert; they were the colour of rain and cloud and the grey of shrubs, and in their hair there were the twigs and nettles and wildflowers.

The women reached out to embrace her but she was frightened. She still carried the poison of the seas. She was still dying. She opened her mouth to speak, certain now that she had seen them, that they would understand her tongue. Overhead, Nyami flapped his wings and watched. She told them what she had come to share. That the sea had turned to poison and would soon ruin the clouds. She told them there was only this left — the sweet water in the middle of the red country.

The women smiled and nodded. They never allowed strangers in, but they could see that Mami Wata was no stranger. They had watched with tired eyes as the skyscrapers went up and the inventions whirred. They had turned into stones when the pale men drove past in their trucks and with their instruments, guarding the source and they had begun to walk when they sensed that the mermaid was near.

There was a healer among them, a woman whose hands were strong and whose gaze was firm. She carried a small sac on her shoulder, a cabinet of medicines. She rubbed herself with oil and asked Mami Wata to come to her. Mami Wata hesitated. She did not want to hurt any of them. Nyami stretched his wings and settled again in the tree, ready to fight with her if need be.

Mami Wata was the last of her kind and she did not die. She had lived to honour the dead in the seas until the oceans had turned against her and now she was fighting to protect the water that had always held her safe. And here in the desert she had arrived and was finally home. Having lost her daughters, she had found her sisters.

The women embraced Mami Wata and her blue-black skin was luminous again. Warmed by the fire and by the ferocity of women, she lay on the ground and allowed herself to be exhausted. Under the care of these women's hands, the seas would return. The water — like her — was immortal.

The Prime Minister

SJ MINNIECON

Prologue
The beloved harsh Australian bush

The heat encompassed his whole being like some huge fiery
band that threatened to crush the very life from his body.
He knew he could not last much longer. Already his mind
had begun to lapse. His feet fumbled once more in the little
sand hollows and he sprawled prostrate for a while on the
sun-scorched plain. Through the numbness of his distressed
mind, there penetrated the shrill cry of Galahs. He struggled
to his feet.

Like wavering ghosts, through the heat haze he saw the
line of trees and with new hope he stumbled on toward the
darkest green, where the squawking flock told him there
was water. The water was warm, brackish, but it caressed
his body with the embrace of new life. Finally, he dragged
his tired body from the small sandy surface-pool and sank

down wearily in the shade of the old river-gums there.

It was as if time had stood still since the accident. His weary mind struggled back to a conversation with his father — when was it? Yesterday? A week, a month ago? The accident and lack of water had confused him, he realized now that he had water and hope again …

Chapter 1
Dad's world

The flickering firelight threw weird patterns upon the screen of night. Across the campfire the vague silhouette of his father's steady voice broke through the clinging tendrils of silence.

'Well son, guess you're glad we're going home again; pretty rough on you out here,' he'd said, looking me over for signs of disquiet.

'Oh no, dad. I've enjoyed myself, it's been a real break,' I'd assured him truthfully. The older man looked directly at him, grinning from ear to ear at the admission.

'It's been a real break for me too son,' he said, handling the lump of metal they'd found, as he spoke. 'A real bit of luck finding something for a change,' he'd said, still overjoyed at finding a decent lump of gold; 'a genuine life-changer', he'd called it.

'Now I've got enough to give you the education I want you to have,' he said happily. 'Smarts like yours should be used for the country son,' he said, always thinking of the broader view of things and always pushing the value of Education as a necessity for all, and not just a great employment tool for rich people's kids; as it seemed to be now.

One thing about dad. He followed his own advice and kept up with all the news and gossip for his own edification about his beloved country. But I was still young and not as certain about education's value as he was. The old man had always encouraged honesty, silly or not, and I'd spoken my youthful doubt aloud.

'Well to be honest dad, I don't think education is everything. You know ...' I began, but was interrupted as dad's abiding passion rose to the fore.

'Perhaps you're right, but I want you to have a good education; the best money can buy. You know I still hope that someday you will hold the reins of Government in this country,' he said, reinforcing the dream he'd had since I showed promise as a child. And, promptly, he was off on his hobby-horse again ...

'The Garden' lies down-under

'This is the greatest country on earth bar none, and this land, our own Queensland, is the Eldorado: the Aladdin's lamp of the Commonwealth,' he said, simplifying his broad, well-read knowledge of international economics. 'But sad to say the genie still lies asleep, because the powers that be suffer from a lack of original ideas,' he expounded. 'We need Statesmen with initiative and drive, and a love for this land,' he said, emotion poking through his usual stolid character. He shook his head gloomily before continuing.

'The patriotic spirit is a negative force in the Australian way of life. Everyone takes life as it comes; its programs, its policies, its privileges are taken for granted. In fact, the whole Government system suffers from an inferiority complex, and you know what that means!' he exclaimed irritably.

'No? What does it mean, dad?' the young man across from him asked seriously.

'Just this boy,' he said, nodding sagely. 'When someone with an inferiority complex is able to get someone weaker down, he not only puts his foot on the victim's neck, but he rubs his nose in the mud as well, and that's what is happening to Australia and its people,' he said disgustedly, gazing into the flames.

'Parliament in Australia is no more than a tourist paradise for the politicians! You get to Parliament and taxpayers pay for your trips around the world,' he spat out, obviously frustrated at the current politicians' attitudes. He wasn't finished.

'Look son! They lay telecommunications cables that cost millions and then go and fly across the Pacific for a few hours talk that costs a lot more money and nobody really knows what they talk about. Could be, they discuss the next winner at Ascot for all we know. They squabble and squall over passing bills for buying toothpicks, to purchasing a turbo-jet,' he said drolly.

'You're sure sore at the Government, aren't you dad!' his son said and laughed.

'Well, son,' his father answered, 'not sore, but sick and fed up to the neck with leaders who bow and scrape, and copy ideas, making mistakes that should never be.'

Being his father's boy, the son brought up humanity as imperfect. 'We all make mistakes though dad? You sound like a 'Commo'!' the boy said, playing 'devil's advocate'.

His father almost snorted. 'Commo be hanged!' he retorted. 'The mistakes are there alright — for all to see! But when it comes to downright bungling … Listen boy, I saw a whole Flying-gang in north Queensland put to work on a short railway line: new rails, new sleepers, new dog-spikes. The Flying-gang had no sooner finished it than the line was closed down and everything was pulled up again!' he said crossly from actual experience of substantial financial and man-power wastage that had irked him greatly.

'Now, who pays for that sort of nonsense? And that's not an isolated case. Plain stupidity I call it!' the older man said flatly.

His son spread his arms in a gesture of helplessness. 'Oh well, what's the use then dad? You're just a voice crying in the wilderness. Nothing we can do to reform them?' he said gloomily.

'That's the trouble boy,' his father said crossly. 'Everybody says the same thing. Everybody thinks the same way: 'we can't do anything!' And so, nothing is tried, and the mudhole grows deeper,' his father simplified.

'Now you sound like a Professor, dad! Guess you've got the solution to it all?' he'd said with a grin. His father grinned along, but answered confidently — he'd obviously put some major thought into the problems his country faced …

Chapter 2

A solution for every problem

'The solution is simple,' his father said. 'It just means work. Work for the development of our country and the welfare of our people,' he explained simply.

'But isn't that what they are doing dad?' the boy asked seriously.

In the flickering light of the low-burning fire his father shook his head negatively. 'I doubt it son! I doubt it very much,' he said, bending to throw a branch on the fire before continuing.

'Just look at it this way. They're spending billions on airplanes which are almost useless and obsolete by the time they're flying. And tell me son, what could an airplane or a hundred airplanes do in a nuclear war? Why! It would be over before they left the ground. Now look here …' his father rose and swung his arm in a wide circle.

'Richmond, Boulia, Birdsville, Camooweal, the 'Alice' and the 'Curry'. A land of far horizons. A good land. The best! All it needs is water. Now go and stand on any of the mountains along the coast, from Rockhampton right up to Cairns, in December through March, and you'll see hundreds of thousands of billions of gallons of water flowing out to sea,' he stated passionately. Across from him, his son spread his arms as he spoke.

'Well I don't see how they can do much about that though dad, do you?' he queried earnestly.

'Of course they can son,' he said, winding up. 'Do you know, if I were an enemy desiring to take North Queensland, I'd just go in and destroy their water supply. It's silly when you think about it. Townsville, the second city, or so they say, has three little lobster holes they call weirs and one two-foot pipeline. A few cases of gelignite and you'd have Townsville in a panic. Same with Cairns,' he explained and continued.

'Now, you travel up the Gillies highway from Gordonvale and look back, you'll see the Mulgrave River flowing a banker most of the year, cutting a path between two mountains maybe less than a mile apart. Now, if they threw a wall across that, there would be enough water and power for all north and west Queensland. They could run pipes over into those western waterways and from then on, well the possibilities are unlimited,' he assured the boy.

'But that would cost a lot of money dad, and even so, they say the evaporation out here is too great for the water to do much good,' he said, remembering a research paper he'd read on the subject.

'Well son, it would cost about as much as one or two of those airplanes they're buying. As for evaporation, all they need to do is bring the ocean down through Cooper's Creek to fill Lake Eyre and keep it filled, and you'd have moisture in the air all the time,' he explained.

The young man shook his head as he thought of something else that his country may need. 'Sure sounds easy dad, but what say we did have an invasion? We would need those planes then,' he stated boldly, causing his father to almost scoff.

'Invasion son? Who's going to invade us, unless it's like Rolf Harris says: 'Turn the Abos loose Bruce and tie me Kangaroos down,' his father said and laughed. 'No son! The Government doesn't want this country to go ahead; they want it for themselves, and I mean themselves,' he said indignantly.

'So long as they can raise their salaries when they want to, go for long trips to the other side of the world when they want; Well! Why worry about anybody else? One year tripping around the world, one year tripping around Australia blowing a lot of hot air, and one year planning their next election campaign,' he mocked.

'You've certainly got a chip on your shoulder dad,' his son said, softening the criticism with a smile. But his father shook his head.

'Not exactly son. All I'm trying to do is show you the picture; and when you get up 'there', you might remember these words and work for your country and your people,' he said optimistically, and winking. 'And you won't fail; you can't,' he said smiling confidently at the flickering uncertain face of his companion.

'You make it sound so positive dad, you'd think I was there already,' his young companion said, amazed as always at his father's passionate visions of national political leadership for himself.

'You will son, you'll get there I'm sure. But come, it's time to turn in now, we have a big day tomorrow. Two, three days we'll be home,' he'd said, unknowing what was in store for them on the morrow ...

At the creek; Alone

However long later — here and now — and his bright-eyed, bright-minded father lay back there in that same beloved land he'd worshipped; in a shallow grave. The only landmarks, a pyramid-shaped rock and a broken twisted jeep to mark his passing.

With life-saving water within and over his parched bruised and battered body, the young man fell asleep, his weariness pushing all thought from his mind as he fell into a deep healing sleep …

Chapter 3
A lifetime later

The beautiful crescent-shaped space liner hung poised gracefully at Space Stage 7. Millions of miles away, her home planet, Earth, shone brilliant; another star in the deep space humanity had begun exploring. The voice of the Captain crackled across to the control tower satellite:

'SL-one set for take-off. Destination planet earth. Thirty-five passengers, all for Earth,' the disembodied voice stated within and without the sleek Space-Liner. A minute later, another disembodied voice responded over a distant alarm sound; the auto-alarm ensuring all staff were clear of the take-off dock:

'SS-seven to SL-one. You are cleared for take-off. You have priority clearance for all docking stations within five minutes. Safe voyage SL-one. SS-seven over and out.' There was a smooth bump as the docking station unlocked and the space-liner hung under its own anti-gravity drive. Moments later the laser tubes glowed. A terrible white light burst for a second from the exhausts and the exquisite craft swept out and on through the vacuum of space on its journey to the home planet.

In one of its luxurious apartments sat two men — one an interstellar reporter, the other, a very old, dignified-looking and well-dressed gentleman. The reporter switched on his com device, tested levels and vid-image and began the interview with his esteemed companion.

'Mr. Prime Minister, can you tell us what impressions have you gained on your interplanetary visits?' he asked.

The older man spoke slowly, carefully measuring his words. 'Well, nothing exceptional really. After all, we on Earth can still show them something since our Equalisor Plan was put into practice,' he said with some evident pride.

The reporter nod and continued. 'Yes, I've heard about the plan, and that you personally had a lot to do in the formation of it. Could you give our listeners a brief description of it perhaps?' he asked …

Chapter 4
A fear exposed

The older man was silent for a while, but the reporter wait patiently, knowing the unique, three-term, octogenarian PM was gathering his thoughts, as he was wont to do before speaking publicly about anything.

'Well, I guess it was the study of the masses that formed the idea. I used to study the people: our people; their reactions in certain circumstances,' he explained slowly into the almost eerie silence of the wonderful craft that bore them home.

'I found that humans in general, despite their often self-centered, negative traits, were really willing and generous in emergencies. This was especially evident in cases of disaster such as flooding, fires or cyclones. You would find they were ready to help in almost every way,' he explained, spreading his arms in a gesture of happy wonder.

'So, I asked myself; why then was there so much bigotry, violence, hatred and such like in normal times?' the aged PM said distractedly, perhaps thinking back on that time of revelation, before he continued. 'Peeling away the layers and getting down to basics, I came to the conclusion that behind it all was a subconscious fear; fear of an unknown future.

This little stumbling block seemed to be a major cause of the opposing negative emotions that our society was in desperate need of,' he said, continuing before the reporter could jump in.

'Look!' he said, in a manner reminiscent of his father's voice. 'The rich accumulated because of it. The poor struck out because of it; fought because of it. We, ah, I, found it was in any and every way, a major part of a violent seething, jumbled mass of anxiety that came out as these negative emotions,' he told the reporter.

'Remove that fear and the rest would take care of itself,' he explained simply, continuing his explanation.

'Now, three things helped us tremendously in this line of thought and action,' he said, holding a steady but skin-wrinkled hand up; one finger up for the first point. 'First there was an upsurge in production in our own Queensland ...' he began.

The reporter, looking confused, interrupted. 'Queensland? Where is that?' he asked never having heard the term before.

The old PM grinned and laughed. 'I'm sorry,' he said, still grinning at using the old name of his home State. 'I still think of it as Queensland, even though they changed the name to Space Central many years ago,' he explained, gaining a nod from the reporter who remembered that name now it was mentioned.

'Anyway, as I said, we had a huge production increase in all spheres of industry including foods, and instead of wasting the surplus as had been done previously by governments, growers, transport and retail, we built those huge plants on our arid, formerly wasted lands and snap-froze all surplus right across the nation,' he told the young reporter, whom had only known such government and entrepreneurial-managed abundance as the norm in his young life.

'What happened then?' the reporter queried, openly curious about the first-hand information from the aged PM.

'Well I think that was then that the plan of equalization began to form,' he explained. 'If everyone had sufficient: same privileges, where he wasn't a slave to work or rather, he never worked for reward but his work was his reward, his chance to expend his energy, to show his ability, it would put his thinking in the right perspectives,' he explained simply.

'Then we travelled our world seeking a working hypothesis. We examined theories of different orders: Democracy, Communism and any other 'ists' and 'isms'. Some were very good in theory but in actual practice they were almost all the same; all lacked something,' he told the reporter.

'Also, the world had reached a great economic crisis: millions were out of work. The world was becoming a desperate place to live in. It almost amounted to survival of the fittest.'

'Sounds terrible,' the reporter interjected, too young to remember the social upheaval of the time.

Chapter 5
Equalisor

'It certainly was,' the old PM agreed wholeheartedly. 'But, as I said before, we had in Queensland, or Space Central as we now call it, reached this peak in production and something had to be done and quickly. We put the Equalisor Plan into practice: first a small community, then towns and cities, until all our own State was working to the Plan,' he explained and nodded at the memory. 'Nothing was wasted. That which was not required at home or for export was either frozen, dehydrated, tinned or cured and everybody had enough. Everybody worked, and willingly, because he knew that whatever was produced was going to benefit his community and his country, himself and his family as well. So, we had the whole State working to the Equalisor system,' he said, obviously proud of the achievement.

'It must have caused an upset to the rest of the country,' the reporter remarked.

The PM grinned cheekily. 'Not only our country, leaders of the whole world were against it. We were completely isolated,' he told the reporter, who thought for a moment before following that line of reasoning to a more personal level.

'How did this affect you?' he asked.

Once again, the old PM grinned. 'Well, not much. Our people were happy and care free. That nagging fear of the future was wiped out. All men were equal, and women too, naturally,' he finished.

'Sounds pretty good to me,' the reporter agreed wholeheartedly.

'It was. Although the world cut us off, they couldn't stop the individual travelers. They came, they saw. Some stayed, some went back and spread the news and soon everyone was wanting to emigrate to Queensland. We were drawing the best brains in the world, and eventually they had to notice. It was then that the other break came from the University of Queensland,' he said, awe still obvious in his aged voice at the huge leap that discovery unleashed.

'Your Antigravity Reactors,' the reporter finished for him; wonder evident in his own voice. The breakthrough had been scientifically stupendous after all; a 'game-changer', the reporter remembered.

The PM smiled warmly. 'Ah! I see that even in Interstellar you have some of our history,' he said, continuing …

Chapter 6
Change gonna come

'It's marvelous! When you take fear from the mind, what wonders it can achieve. You see we gradually got away from old standards. Instead of gold standards we made production standards. The old bits of paper and coins we'd used were completely finished with, and in so doing, we'd done away with old vices: stealing, lying, sickness was rare; murder and robbery were very, very rare,' he explained and rushed on, animated by the memories.

'Work became a pastime and pleasure. Old modes of transport became obsolete; old four-wheeled vehicles called motorcars that were a grave source of danger but a necessity in those days, were placed on scrap heaps and recycled. Old buildings of iron and steel and concrete were done away with and new types of plastics were used instead. Men were taught to see that safety instead of antique design and ideas was much more desirable,' he told the reporter, who held up a finger.

'By the way, what are those iron and, what was it? Con-crete? And steel things you mentioned?' he asked not knowing the terms.

'Oh well, they were heavy, cumbersome materials that could maim and kill when they collapsed,' he explained quickly. 'However,' he said, eager to continue, 'to get back to our story, the Antigravity reactor gave us a great lead over the nations, followed quickly by the laser-tube drive. The world began to take notice and adopt our plans,' he said softly but proudly.

'That must have been a great day,' said the reporter.

The PM smiled again. 'A real Jubilee day now; as a matter of fact, I'll just be in time for the Jubilee celebrations,' the PM said happily.

'And is that all the Equalisor plan has done?' the reporter queried, knowing there was much more to the plan.

'Far from all,' the Prime Minister answered. 'We were then able to go forward with our plans for a greater Earth,' he said, obviously thinking back to those days.

'Would you please explain, Mr. Prime Minister?' the reporter duly asked.

'Well, we'd formed a plan in our universities of placing manmade suns, coupled to Antigravity reactors of course, above our polar regions. They were huge mirror-like devices orbiting our poles that absorbed and reflected the rays and heat of our main sun that just rose above the horizon during summer months in those polar regions. This proved a real success. A deal of ice and snow were melted and the surplus water was drained into our deserts, and in this we had full control,' he told the reporter, taking a deep breath to continue …

Chapter 7
Hidden treasures

'And what a wealth of treasure lay hidden beneath the ice and snow, and millions more acres of really productive land, especially in our North Pole; enough for many generations,' he explained, sipping water for a parched throat. 'The South Pole was largely very deep caverns, but still a whole new wonderland; the geologist's dream, the archaeologist's playground,' he said, pausing for breath.

'It's small wonder then that you are so honoured among the planets,' the newsman remarked. 'But you've only given me the natural physical side: how does the plan affect people, say… ah? morally?' he asked, knowing his listeners would be similarly wondering at that aspect of the plan.

The old man sat silent for a long time, his fingers tapping gently on the table-top. At last, he answered. 'It has taken many long years of careful study to remove and keep on removing all the obstacles in the way of equality in the moral make-up of the human,' he said slowly. 'Again, we had to find a new, quite possibly more difficult working hypothesis,' he began to explain.

The reporter nodded enthusiastically, drawing the tale out.

'Basically, to the huge majority, religion was found to be the deciding factor in the moral make-up; marriage, the home life, the family, the community and so on,' the PM said, remembering the research. 'So, we investigated religion in all its forms,' he said, as if it was a normal Government action; a duty even.

'We found there were literally thousands of religious beliefs and ideas, and these thousands meant thousands of gaps in human society, and these gaps were the hardest to bridge,' he said softly, lost in thought for a moment.

'Some are not yet fully filled, but we investigated until it finally came to one focal point. It all reached out to a God, a power above all human societies,' he explained, pausing again to sip water and rubbing his hands together as he continued his train of thought.

'The rich, the poor, the learned, the ignorant, the civilized, the barbarians; everyone sought it in some form or other, but the crucial point was that each section — or whatever you want to call it — wanted it or Him for their own little tin God, to take him to this church or that, to set him up as idols or images, until the whole became just a stupid distorted meaningless mass of hysteria,' he exclaimed passionately.

'And we had to find a solution, a working hypothesis. Here again we came across a simple solution, a book called The Bible,' he explained. 'It started out with a declaration that God, this Power everyone was seeking, made the world. Thus, a living universe, a living planet and a living God. To us, this was logical and sensible, so we investigated this book further,' he said, looking directly at the reporter.

'And, did you find anything worthwhile?' he was asked.

The Prime Minister smiled humbly. 'It proved the most engrossing book I've ever read,' he stated. 'Its thoughts and words were tremendously powerful, personal and practical for honest, dignified daily living,' he said, nodding confidently. 'I think the declaration that 'this' God or Power, had reproduced Himself in man is what first caught my attention; and caused me to read and study this particular book,' he said, catching the reporter's eye once more.

'It had a profound effect on my own life, so profound that I sought to promote it to be read and studied in schools and universities in an effort to solve the religion problem in their search for this God,' he told the reporter.

'And have you found Him?' the newsman asked cheekily.

For answer the old man flicked a switch on the desk between them. On the wall, a screen rolled back and one of the ship's Astro-scanners swung into view. Through the inky purple blackness, the Earth's sun hung: a golden orb. Farther out, the Milky Way swept across the heavens like some beautiful silver-studded archway spread over with diamond dust. Pluto, Venus, Saturn, Sirius; all silvered jewels in a purple robe.

Both remained silent as the space-liner rushed on through that gem-studded arch. Then the old man quoted: 'The heavens declare the glory of God and the firmament showeth His handiwork,' he intoned.

With a sardonic grin, the reporter said: 'That doesn't prove a thing. You haven't found this 'God', you haven't seen Him,' he said self-assuredly to the PM's budding grin.

A raised finger accompanied the response. 'Ah, but we have Mr. Reporter, we have. Only glimpses as yet, but they're glimpses all the same,' he responded cheerily to the man's obvious doubt.

'Where? How?' the reporter asked immediately. The old PM's eyes smiled, a new light deep within as he responded.

'In happy, healthy, thriving, contented towns, cities, communities and country where every man's hand is outstretched to help his neighbour, and further yet across continents, across oceans; black hands, white hands, yellow hands, brown hands, stretched out in peace and goodwill among men,' he said buoyantly as Earth grew steadily larger in the Astro-scanner …

Epilogue
Revisiting the beginning

The evening shadows were blending into dusk as the old man walked slowly along the shore of the vast, man-made inland sea. A successful project from out of his father's fervent mind. For a moment he stood and gazed out to where huge Evacuums lifted the water thousands of feet into the air, then sprayed it out in fine clouds that floated away on the evening breeze.

Behind him the wind whispered fragrantly through the tall forests of pines, while herds of cattle lay quietly or roamed through the tall grass. The aged man turned and walked slowly on through the dusk. A tall, pyramid-shaped stone loomed up out of the shadows. Beside it rusted and paper-thin but still recognizable, lay a twisted broken Jeep.

Here, the night winds whispered: 'Boulia, Birdsville, Camooweal, The Alice, a land of far horizons' …

The old man lifted his eyes to where the Evening Star shone brightly, then slowly, reverently, he took off his beaten, sweat-stained old hat and stood with bowed head.

A Note from the Family of Uncle SJ Minniecon

'My father didn't have any opportunity to go to school and get a quality education because he was raised under the oppressive apartheid Queensland Aboriginal Protection Act. Yet, in spite of the oppression and restrictions forced upon him, he taught himself to read and write. He also wrote a collection of poems and left us a number of our language songs and stories. He taught us by example. He inspired us by example that education is accessible, no matter what the racial, legal and social barriers.' — Pastor Ray Minniecon

A Note from the Editors

This visionary work was created long before we were born. It was created at a time when First Nations people on this continent were not seen or treated as human beings. We are privileged and humbled to have the permission to publish this piece, it has been published as original with no edits. We thank the family of Uncle SJ Minniecon for this chance. We end this work remembering that no work of visionary fiction was ever created in a vacuum. Our elders and ancestors began a journey on which we are merely adding a page, in hopes for more just futures.

Biographical Notes

Tuesday Atzinger is a poet and emerging writer. Their work explores and celebrates Afro-blackness, queerness, disability and feminism. They peddle in discomfort and their primary goal is to fling words together to make you squirm. They have performed spoken word for the Melbourne Writers Festival and Melbourne Fringe. When they aren't feverishly building a lexicon of words that rhyme, they can be found online, using Twitter badly. They live and work on the unceded lands of the Wurundjeri People of the Kulin Nations.

Flora Chol is Melbourne based South Sudanese writer, poet and community activist. In 2003 Flora arrived in Australia with her mother and siblings as a refugee through the United Nations Humanitarian program. Flora is a passionate community advocate who dedicates her time to working in the South Sudanese community, in particular the education and youth services sector. Flora is currently completing her Master of International Community Development at Deakin University and writing her first children's book.

Claire G Coleman is a Noongar woman whose family have belonged to the south coast of Western Australia since before history started being recorded. Growing up near Boorloo, now living in the hills near Naarm she writes fiction, non-fiction, drama and verse. She has published three novels and a non-fiction book. Claire has also written for many publications including *Meanjin, The Saturday Paper, The Guardian, Australian Poetry, Griffith Review, Chicago Review* and *Spectrum.*

Zena Cumpston is a Barkandji woman with family connection to Broken Hill and Menindee in western New South Wales. She currently lives in Melbourne on the lands of the Wurundjeri people with her partner and two young boys. Zena is a writer, curator, consultant, academic, educator and researcher. In 2021 she curated the show 'Emu Sky' for Science Gallery Melbourne, exploring Aboriginal knowledge and bringing together over 30 Aboriginal community members, sharing their stories, research, knowledge and art works. Zena is passionate about truth-telling and undertaking projects that directly benefit Aboriginal community. In 2022 her book *Plants*, written with Wiradjuri academic Associate Professor Michael-Shawn Fletcher and Professor Lesley Head, will be published as part of the 'First Knowledges' series.

Lisa Fuller is a Wuilli Wuilli woman from Eidsvold, Queensland, also descended from Wakka Wakka and

Gooreng Gooreng peoples. She is currently doing her PhD in Creative Writing at the University of Canberra. Lisa won a 2019 black&write! Fellowship, the 2017 David Unaipon Award for an Unpublished Indigenous Writer, the 2018 Varuna Eleanor Dark Flagship Fellowship and a 2018 Copyright Agency Fellowship for First Nations Writers. Her debut novel, *Ghost Bird*, has won numerous awards. Lisa wears many hats in pursuit of her writing, including sessional academic, freelance writer, editor and publishing consultant.

Meleika Gesa-Fatafehi AKA Vika Mana is pretty hilarious and laughs too much, so much that her Black/Indigenous and Pasifika ancestors are probably tired of her. Luckily, she alternates burdening the two sides of her ancestry who are from Mer (Murray) Island, from the Zagareb and Dauareb tribes and Tonga, from the village Fahefa. She loves talking about all things nerdy, as well as decolonising spaces online and in real life. She a sovereign storyteller that writes, creates, films and records their stories to share with the world. They hope to one day direct and film a documentary of their home on Mer. If she's upset any of her ancestors whilst making this bio, she's sorry.

Dr Vivienne Glance and Afeif Ismail have been collaborating for nearly two decades on co-transcreating his writing from Arabic to English. Vivienne Glance is also a poet, playwright and performer.

Chemutai Glasheen is Kenyan born and now lives in Western Australia. She is a teacher and a sessional academic at Curtin University. She writes fiction for young people and her work is influenced by her interest and experience in human rights and education. She has written a collection of short stories which are set in east Africa. Her work has been published in *ACE: Arresting Contemporary stories by Emerging writers* and in the Museum of Freedom and Tolerance website.

Genevieve Grieves is a proud Worimi woman, with more than twenty years' experience creating dynamic content for film and television, exhibitions, online and multimedia. Her work has consistently won awards and recognition and she is regarded as a leading practitioner of community-engaged content development. She is a passionate advocate of these practices and teaches in university, institutional and community spaces, as well as mentoring many emerging First Peoples creatives. She was the Lead Curator of the internationally celebrated permanent exhibition, First Peoples at Melbourne Museum.

Hella Ibrahim is the founder and editorial director of Djed Press, an online publication that provides a paid platform for creators of colour, and is an editor with a passion for activism through writing and publishing.

Afeif Ismail is an award-winning Australian–Sudanese writer. He is an internationally published poet and playwright whose works have been translated into German, Spanish and Swedish. Afeif has published six of poetry collections in Arabic as well as a short story collection.

Rafeif Ismail, who identifies as a third-culture youth of the Sudanese diaspora, is an award-winning emerging author committed to creating accessible spaces for young people of marginalised backgrounds in the Arts.

Ambelin Kwaymullina belongs to the Palyku people of the eastern Pilbara region of Western Australia. She is a writer, illustrator and law academic who works across a range of genres including YA, science fiction, verse and non-fiction. She is a previous winner of the Victorian Premier's Literary Award and the Aurealis Award.

Laniyuk is a Larrakia, Kungarakan, Gurindji and French writer and performer of poetry and short memoir. She contributed to the book *Colouring the Rainbow: Blak, Queer and Trans Perspectives*, has been published online and in print poetry collections. She received Canberra's Noted Writers Festival's 2017 Indigenous Writers Residency, Overland's 2018 Writers Residency and was shortlisted for Overland's 2018 Nakata-Brophy poetry prize. She is currently completing her first collection of work to be published through Magabala Books.

Jenna Lee is a Gulumerridjin (Larrakia), Wardaman and KarraJarri Saltwater woman with mixed Japanese, Chinese, Filipino and Anglo-Australian ancestry. Formally trained as a graphic designer, she works independently specialising in book cover design, exhibition identity design and print design for the arts sector as well as being a practising visual artist.

Jasmin McGaughey is a Torres Strait Islander and African American writer and editor. She has completed a Master of Writing Editing and Publishing at the University of Queensland and is in the midst of a Master of Philosophy in creative writing. In 2019, she was a black&write! editor intern and won a Wheeler Centre The Next Chapter Fellowship. She has written for *Overland, Kill Your Darlings, SBS Voices* and *Griffith Review.*

Sterling James Minniecon (1918–2006) was from the Kabi Kabi Nation of South-East Queensland and a descendant of the South Sea Islander people of Ambrym Island, Vanuatu. SJ Minniecon was the first Aboriginal pastor to be appointed under the Assemblies of God. He taught himself to read and write, and was the author of poetry and speculative fiction.

Sisonke Msimang writes about belonging. She is the author of two books, and has been published in a wide range of publications including the *New York Times, Guernica Magazine* and *Newsweek.* She is the winner of the

2020 Western Australian Premier's Book Awards Writer's Fellowship.

Merryana Salem is a proud Wonnarua and second-generation Lebanese–Australian author, culture writer, teacher, and podcaster. They are the co-creator and co-host of the LGBT media podcast, GayV Club, and a regular contributor and staff writer for *The Big Issue, Kill Your Darlings* and *Junkee*. In 2021, she was shortlisted for the Penguin Random House Write It Fellowship. Find them on Twitter @akajustmerry.

Mykaela Saunders is a Koori writer, teacher and community researcher, and the editor of *This All Come Back Now*, the world's first anthology of blackfella speculative fiction, forthcoming with University of Queensland Press in 2022. Of Dharug and Lebanese descent, and working-class and queer, Mykaela belongs to the Tweed Goori community. Mykaela's fiction, poetry, essays and research has won the Elizabeth Jolley Short Story Prize, the National Indigenous Story Award, the Oodgeroo Noonuccal Indigenous Poetry Prize, the Grace Marion Wilson Emerging Non-fiction Writers Prize and the University of Sydney's Sister Alison Bush Graduate Medal for Indigenous research. More information can be found at mykaelasaunders.com

Aïsha Trambas is an Afro-Greek arts worker based on Wurundjeri and Boonwurrung land. She is interested in becoming more herself, and figuring out what she's meant to be doing here. These endeavours take shape through Aïsha's various practices in writing, visual art, zine-making, facilitation and event production. Aïsha was the Program Coordinator of the Emerging Writers' Festival in 2019, and has performed at Yirramboi Festival, Melbourne Writers' Festival and Melbourne Fringe.

Ellen van Neerven is an award-winning writer, editor and educator of Mununjali Yugambeh and Dutch heritage with strong ancestral ties to south-east Queensland.

Alison Whittaker is a Gomeroi poet, essayist and legal academic.

Yirga Gelaw Woldeyes is a writer, researcher and poet from Lalibela, Ethiopia. He currently lives in Perth, Western Australia, where he is a Senior Lecturer at the Centre for Human Rights Education, Curtin University. His academic and creative work revolves around African traditions, Ethiopian philosophy, epistemic justice, issues of looted manuscript repatriation, and the politics of language and belonging. His Amharic poetry was published in a solo collection, and has been performed widely on stage and radio in Ethiopia. His English creative work has appeared in *Westerly, Stories of Perth* and *Ways of Being Here.*

Jasper Wyld is a descendant of the Martu people of Western Australia. In 2019, they were one of the recipients of The Wheeler Centre's mentorship and manuscript development scheme, The Next Chapter. They are currently in the process of writing a series of fantasy novels.

Maree McCarthy Yoelu is a Wadjigany woman, from the western Wagait region in the Northern Territory. Maree is a children's author. She lives in Darwin with her family, where she works in radio and continues to write stories connected to her people and culture.

First published 2022 by
FREMANTLE PRESS in association with Djed Press

DJED PRESS

Reprinted 2024.

Fremantle Press Inc. trading as Fremantle Press
PO Box 158, North Fremantle, Western Australia, 6159
fremantlepress.com.au

Cover design by Jenna Lee.

A catalogue record for this
book is available from the
National Library of Australia

ISBN 9781760990701 (paperback)
ISBN 9781760991463 (ebook)

Fremantle Press is supported by the Western Australian State Government
through the Department of Cultural Industries, Tourism and Sport.

This project has been assisted by the Australian Government
through the Australia Council, its arts funding and advisory body.

Fremantle Press respectfully acknowledges the Whadjuk people of the
Noongar nation as the traditional owners and custodians of the land
where we work in Walyalup.

www.ingramcontent.com/pod-product-compliance
Lightning Source LLC
Chambersburg PA
CBHW020538020726
47494CB00006B/1818